MESSAGE OF LOVE

MESSAGE OF LOVE

Rose Swan

Chivers Press • G.K. Hall & Co.
Bath, England   Thorndike, Maine USA

This Large Print edition is published by Chivers Press, England, and by G.K. Hall & Co., USA.

Published in 2001 in the U.K. by arrangement with Robert Hale Ltd.

Published in 2001 in the U.S. by arrangement with Robert Hale Ltd.

U.K. Hardcover ISBN 0-7540-4393-2 (Chivers Large Print)
U.K. Softcover ISBN 0-7540-4394-0 (Camden Large Print)
U.S. Softcover ISBN 0-7838-9336-1 (Nightingale Series Edition)

The text of this Large Print edition is unabridged.
Other aspects of the book may vary from the original edition.

Set in 16 pt. New Times Roman.

Printed in Great Britain on acid-free paper.

British Library Cataloguing in Publication Data available

Library of Congress Cataloging-in-Publication Data

Swan, Rose.
      Message of love / by Rose Swan.
          p. cm.
      ISBN 0-7838-9336-1 (lg. print : sc : alk. paper)
      1. Guardian and ward—Fiction. 2. Kidnapping—Fiction.
      3. Sri Lanka—Fiction. I. Title.
      PR6069.W343 M47 2001
      823'.92—dc21   00–053901

CHAPTER ONE

Patsy looked across the room through the slightly dusty windows at the almond tree which was just breaking into pale pink blossom in the garden. For a moment her mind was distracted from the children who played at her feet until a voice announced angrily, 'Peter's got a piece of my puzzle and he won't give it back!' Hastily she crouched down beside the two little boys on the floor and showed Peter that indeed the piece of board he was so firmly clutching didn't belong to the puzzle he was doing. She watched, helping slightly, until the simple puzzles were finished, and then she called all the children to sit at her feet while she told them a story. From time to time as she repeated one of the old favourites they usually demanded, her eyes strayed to the pink buds on the black branches, and the blue sky beyond. Spring had come so suddenly, she thought; last week she had been buttoning these nursery-school children into coats, and finding matching gloves before their mothers picked them up; now most of them were just wearing cardigans and no gloves were in evidence.

'You said it wrong!' a little voice complained reproachfully, again dragging her back to her surroundings. 'You should say he had a huge

1

black horse, not a big black horse.'

'I'm sorry, Billy.' Patsy smiled down at the earnest young face. 'That was silly of me. He did have a huge black horse, and it danced and pranced and its bridle jingled.'

'That's right.' Billy was content again and as she went on with a story she had told so many times before, Patsy's eyes were soft, and she watched with affection the various expressions which chased themselves across the little faces fixed on hers. They knew every word of all their favourite stories, and someone always complained if she deviated by so much as a word. Resolutely she kept her mind on the story, and then on their questions and chatter as they prepared to be collected and taken home. She chatted with one or two of the mothers, waved goodbye to the children, and then sank into her chair and just stared into space.

Sue, her friend and co-worker, came briskly through from the adjoining room. 'Anything wrong?' she asked, hardly pausing for an answer. 'You tired? I'm all ready to go. Want me to help you to tidy up?'

'No thanks,' Patsy smiled. 'The children have done most of it.'

'I'll wait for you.'

'No—I've got a few things to do. I'll just potter around and then catch the next bus. You go on.'

'OK, I will then. I'm meeting Peter at six,

and I want to wash my hair. Sure you're all right?'

'Sure,' Patsy replied firmly. 'I just feel restless and lazy at the same time. Spring fever, I guess. Only yesterday, it seems, it was winter, and now there are buds on the trees, and daffodils everywhere—'

'—and spring sales,' her friend finished. 'Todds are starting theirs tomorrow, will you come with me after school?'

'Yes, I will,' Patsy agreed. 'There's nothing I specially want, but I can help you to choose.'

'Bet you'll buy something,' Sue declared with a wise grin. 'Well, I'm off then. See you tomorrow.'

When the door had banged behind Sue, and the clatter of her high heels on the path had died away, Patsy still sat on, staring into space. The sight of the pink almond blossom had roused in her a desire to—to what? She couldn't analyse it, but as she had said to Sue, she felt restless and lazy at the same time; but only lazy about doing the same old things. She thought, 'I'd like to do something exciting, go somewhere different, have something new to think about.' Sternly she put these thoughts aside, and getting to her feet—she tidied away a few things and made preparations for the next morning. Then she locked the door behind her and walked slowly to the bus-stop.

She did love her work with the small children in the nursery, she told herself, and

3

for two years she had been perfectly happy there, enjoying each day to the full, and having a real love for her tiny charges. Why then did she suddenly feel that she wanted a change? She looked back over the twenty-three years of her life. As a child she had always been convinced that she wanted to be a nurse, and as soon as she was able to she had flung herself with joyful intensity into her nurse's training. Her father, much older than his wife, had died when Patsy was a young child, and she scarcely remembered him. She had not realised until she was older what a struggle it had been for her not over-strong mother to raise a child on her own. Patsy had never lacked for anything, that she could remember. Clothes, toys, birthday parties, visits to the seaside, all these she had had in common with little friends who had attended the same small private school. Her mother had upheld her decision to become a nurse, and then had understood and comforted Patsy when in tears just over two years later, she had confessed that she wanted to give it all up. The training had been fun, even the hard menial work, and the rigid rules and strict matrons had been fun shared with the other girls. Patsy had sailed easily through all the examinations, and was popular with staff and patients alike for her cheerfulness and her gentleness; but it was this very gentleness that had been her undoing. More and more she had identified herself with her patients, their suffering had become hers, and Matron had chided her several times for being too subjective, before Patsy, grieving over the death of a young boy brought in after a motor-cycle accident, had reluctantly but bravely decided that she would never make a good nurse. In tears she had explained all this to her mother, who had comforted her, told her she was still young, and could choose another career, and urged her to have a little time doing nothing before she made a second choice. Matron had accepted her resignation gravely, but had agreed that Patsy was doing the right thing. 'You can apply to me at any time for a reference,' she offered, 'and, my dear, think about working with people, children perhaps. I think you would be happier doing that than working in an office or something like that.'

Patsy had thought over her advice and followed it, and after a further year of training, this time to be a nursery-school teacher, she had at once found this job conveniently near to home, and happily filling her days. She had been at the school only two terms when her mother had died of complications after what had seemed a simple operation, and the following weeks had been filled with sorrow and many difficult decisions. The family solicitor, who had also been an old friend of her father's, had helped her enormously. 'There is very little money,' he told her gravely, looking at her over steepled fingers. 'The annuity dies with your mother; but there is the house, which I would advise you to sell. It's too big for you alone, it's been too big for you for years, but your mother wanted to keep it because she'd been there all her married life and it had very happy memories.' He had waited for her to speak, but Patsy, still numbed by events, was silent. 'You could invest the money,' he went on. 'It would produce an income, and it would be useful to have the capital if you want to buy a house later, or a smaller house now, or travel, or—' His voice had died away and Patsy had tried to pull herself together and be businesslike. 'C-could you handle it all for me, Mr Phelps?' she had asked. 'I'll try to find a small flat to rent now perhaps, or lodgings somewhere, and I'll carry on with my job and later on decide what I want to do.'

'That's very wise,' he agreed. 'I'll certainly see to everything and keep you informed. Meanwhile, if you like, I'll give you a note to young John Braddly the estate agent. His father was a friend of mine and of your father's. He might be able to put you in the way of finding somewhere to live.'

So it had happened, and so through the death of her mother she had met John. Right from the start it had felt as if they'd known each other for years, though neither could ever remember having met the other before.

'Mother didn't have much social life,' Patsy told him. 'After father died she preferred to be at home; and I suppose you were away at boarding-school.'

'And then at Cambridge,' he agreed, 'but I'm very glad I've met you now.'

After a few weeks he had found her a tiny flat on the outskirts of the town. 'Everywhere in Lynn itself gets snapped up before it's hardly free,' he explained. 'This is the top half of a house just outside, on the road to Wootton, but there's a very good bus service.'

'I still have the car anyhow,' she told him, 'but it's quite difficult to park all day by the school, so I'll be glad of a nearby bus-stop.'

'The house is being bought by a young married couple,' John went on. 'They've got a mortgage and they've decided that until they want to start a family they'll let the top half to help finances. They've put in a small kitchenette, and there is a bathroom and two other rooms.' He took her to see the flat and its owners, a cheerful young couple, both of whom were teachers at the local grammar school. Patsy had taken it and soon settled in, gradually getting used to living alone, and sometimes glad of nearby company. John stayed in her life as if it were the most natural thing in the world. He helped her to move in and advised her about insurance and various other things, and without conscious agreement, they seemed to be always together.

They liked the same things, read the same books, played tennis together, and generally found themselves totally compatible. After just over a year they both assumed that they would eventually marry. John had never asked her to marry him, but gradually into their chat came mentions of 'when we are married'. Sometimes Patsy wondered how on earth she would have dragged herself through those first forlorn miserable months without John, and she blessed Mr Phelps for having introduced him to her.

'We could go on living here,' he had suggested one night when she had cooked for him and they had just finished watching a film on television. 'It would be lovely just to go to bed instead of driving ten miles home in the cold.' Patsy had blushed, but had agreed that at the moment the flat would be fine for them both.

'You wouldn't want to give up working as soon as we're married, would you?' he had continued, 'and we don't want to start a family just yet.' Patsy didn't answer. She had thought of married life as a new beginning, and not just a more intimate continuation of the life they lived now. John had once or twice suggested that a more intimate life would be possible now, and that he needn't always leave to drive himself home. For reasons she hardly understood Patsy had always demurred.

'Your mother would wonder why you didn't

come home,' she murmured, and John had laughed.

'Darling, I'm twenty-eight. There have been lots of nights when I didn't go home. Mother understands. She doesn't worry.' Patsy had fallen silent, imagining John with other women, and he had given her a quick hug.

'But that's all over now,' he assured her, 'for me now there's only you. So let me stay, love.'

'But she would know where you were,' said Patsy, unconsciously contradicting her earlier objection.

'OK, love, I won't rush you,' John had declared, to her secret relief, 'but you'll have to marry me soon. I can't wait for ever.'

'I will,' she promised, but it was not mentioned again except for vague references about 'when we are married'. She had met John's mother and liked her very much, even though she was the very opposite of Patsy's own mother. She too was a widow, but unlike Patsy's mother she lived a very full social life. She played bridge and canasta regularly, she was a very active member of the Townswomen's Guild, and she went regularly to the theatre and to see the latest films. As far as Patsy could tell, John's mother did not approve or disapprove of her—she was just busy leading her own life. 'At least,' Patsy thought, 'she will not be lonely when John moves out.'

Today, as she waited for the bus which

would drop her almost at her own doorstep, Patsy thought of the time when John would move out of his mother's house and in with her. When would it be? In the summer, she supposed; the summer was a good time for weddings; although often in the summer the weather was not as good as it was being today. She thought briefly about the ceremony. If she had ever really thought about it before she had imagined a wedding with all the usual ceremony and trimmings. A wonderful dress, pretty bridesmaids, a reception, speeches, and then a honeymoon to remember for a lifetime. All this, she realised, as she sat in the jolting bus and watched the dust motes dancing in the sunlight, had just been a vague dream, such, she supposed, as most girls must have from time to time. Now she thought of the reality. She was alone in the world except for an aunt, an older sister of her mother's, who lived in Yorkshire. Who would arrange her wedding? Who would give her away? Where would she find the pretty bridesmaids? She had a few casual friends in their early twenties, but only one was married and had a small daughter, and that daughter was not yet a year old. Who would make speeches except John and the best man? Suddenly she felt as alone as she had felt in the first few months after her mother's death. 'We'll have to be married in a registry office,' she thought; 'after all, the marriage is the important thing, not where it actually takes place, nor the window-dressing.'

A young mother got on to the bus carrying a fat baby and a shopping-basket, and with a toddler clinging to her skirt. The conductor obligingly folded her pushchair and pushed it under the stairs, and Patsy steadied the little boy as the bus lurched on its way again, and the girl sank into the only vacant seat, which was next to Patsy.

'Thanks!' she breathed with a smile as she put her basket firmly between her feet. 'Shopping certainly is a pain these days.' She held firmly on to the baby, and then to her young son who stood wedged between them.

'I'll have him on my knee if he'll come,' Patsy offered. 'Have you far to go?'

'Wolverstone, so thank goodness I can sit still for a little while before I have to struggle off again. And Jamie is very friendly, he'll sit on anyone's knee.'

'I'm getting off at Wootton,' Patsy told her, 'and then you can have the whole seat.' She lifted the unprotesting child on to her knee and he leaned his head back against her shoulder. His mother smiled at him tenderly. 'He hates shopping as much as I do,' she remarked. They chatted desultorily for the next few miles until they reached Patsy's destination, and then she sat him on her seat and bade them goodbye.

She and John had never really seriously discussed having children, and she realised suddenly that she knew nothing of his true feelings on the subject. She herself loved children, and had never felt so happy in her life nor so fulfilled since she had been working in the nursery school; but somehow, sitting in the close confines of the bus, hemmed in as it were by two small children, the seeds of sudden doubt were born. Sometimes at the end of a tiring day she'd heaved a sigh of relief as the last mother had led away the last toddler. Children of your own were for twenty-four hours a day; was she ready for that? She'd have to discuss it with John, but already, she thought a little impatiently, she knew what he would say. 'We'll do anything you want, sweetheart.' It was never really possible to discuss anything with John. He was solid and dependable, and always willing to fall in with anything that she suggested. Sometimes she wished that he were not always so amenable. She didn't want to quarrel with him of course, not like Sue and her Pete, who seemed to thrive on fierce rows and equally fierce reconciliations. Patsy couldn't imagine quarrelling with John, but it would be good, stimulating, sometimes to discuss things about which they had different opinions, or to do something different and unexpected. 'It's almost as if we've been married for years and years, and know each other like hand and glove so that nothing is ever new,' she thought, and the restlessness which had possessed her

12

all day rushed back with full force. 'I don't want it to be like that,' she thought. 'I've seen nothing much and done nothing much; I don't want to have already settled into a rut that I'm going to stay in for the rest of my life.' With her mind in chaos she walked the few yards to the house, called a greeting to Jan and Peter, her landlords, who were standing by the side door, and went up to her little flat. While she waited for the kettle to boil for tea, she thought again of John who would undoubtedly come or phone as soon as he closed his office at six. 'He'll say "Hallo, Pats" and I shall feel as irritable about it as I always do.' She thought, 'I wish he wouldn't shorten my name like that, but he always apologises and then does it again.' She got herself a cup of tea and checked that there was food for two in her tiny refrigerator and larder. 'I suppose we'll eat and watch TV,' she thought. 'I wish—' Her thoughts trailed away. What did she wish? Suddenly she felt trapped. The whole countryside around her was bursting with new and vibrant life, and she was going on with the same old day-to-day routine, with nothing much different to look forward to. 'I wish something exciting would happen.' She completed her thought, 'but what that's exciting is likely to happen to me?' She realised with a little shock that she no longer thought of marriage to John as exciting. If she really thought about it, it seemed like an end rather than a beginning. She sat following this dismal train of thought while her tea grew cold. 'It's not just spring fever,' she thought. 'I know now that I've felt like this for a long time; this feeling of dullness and of being— well yes, of being trapped. I've never been out for any length of time with any other boy, and John and I have just drifted towards marriage; but I can't do it. I can't tie myself down yet. John is a darling and life with him would be easy and predictable, but that's not what I want.' Having once admitted these strong feelings to herself, Patsy realised that she must do something about them. She must at least tell John. It was not fair to him just to go on drifting in the hopes that her feelings would change. The phone rang, startling her, and John's cheerful voice was almost like an answer to her thoughts. 'I've got to eat at home with mother tonight,' he said. 'She wants advice about some papers or other that she has to sign, but I'll come over at around nine, OK?'

'OK,' she answered mechanically, 'and John—there's something I want to tell you; to talk about.'

CHAPTER TWO

Patsy put the phone down with a little catch in her breath. She had taken the first step, and now there could be no going back. For a moment she felt panic. What would she do without John? She could find something else to tell him and life could go on as before; but having once admitted to herself that life with John was not what she really wanted, Patsy knew that she could not go back. 'Besides, it would be so unfair to him,' she thought. 'I've got to tell him how I feel. Perhaps we could have a period apart; perhaps—' Her thoughts trailed away as she realised that she didn't want just a period apart and then a return to the same situation. She wanted a new start. 'I guess I just clung to John as a sort of substitute for mother,' she admitted to herself. 'Somehow, having someone always there filled the gap. I've been very unfair to him, and I must put things right.'

Restlessly she prowled around the little flat waiting for John's arrival. How would he take it, she wondered. What would he say? With a near-hysterical giggle she thought that for once he wouldn't say, 'Well do anything you want, sweetheart.' She made herself a sandwich and neglected to eat it. She dusted things that didn't need dusting, and made

15

small rearrangements to the furniture. The clock hands seemed to creep round so slowly. Would nine o'clock never come? She realised with a little shock that she had never before waited so anxiously for John. It was a little before nine when she heard his car outside and she jumped to her feet and stood with her hands clasped nervously in front of her.

John came in with his usual smile and a cry of, 'Hallo, Pats!' which somehow slightly strengthened her resolve. He didn't seem to notice that anything was wrong, and gave her a quick hug before flopping into his usual armchair. 'Any coffee going?' he asked.

'Yes, of course,' she replied and walked through to the tiny kitchen. John's voice followed her, telling bits about his day at the office and a house he thought that perhaps he had sold at last. She came back with the coffee on a tray and began to pour. 'That old place has been on our books for nearly two years,' he went on. 'It'll be great if the sale goes through, and I have a feeling it will. It's someone just back from India with a fancy for an old country house, and the money to indulge his fancy.' Patsy murmured something appropriate and handed him his coffee.

'Thanks, love.' He took the steaming cup from her and took a cautious sip. 'How was your day?'

Patsy took a deep breath. 'Oh, the same as usual,' she said, and then in a rush, 'John.

There's something I want to talk to you about.'

'Oh yes. You said on the phone,' he recalled. 'What is it?' He put down the cup and fumbled for his cigarettes.

There was a small silence as she struggled to find the right words to begin. At last he sensed that she was uneasy. 'What is it, love?' he asked. 'Bad news?'

'Yes. No. I don't know.'

'Well, it can't be all that bad,' John said cheerfully. 'Come on. Tell me all about it.'

Anything that Patsy had thought of saying went out of her head and turning to face him she rushed into speech. 'We've been going out together for a long time now, John,' she began, 'and I know that also for a long time we've assumed that we would marry. Well—I'm sorry, John, but I—I don't want to marry you. I—' She had his full attention now, but to her surprise he was smiling.

'Well, that's nothing to be so solemn about,' he said, reaching for her hand. 'Lots of people don't get married these days. Nobody is shocked, it just doesn't seem to matter. I can just move in here and everything will be all right.' Patsy stared at him.

'But it won't,' she cried. 'You don't understand. I don't want to marry you, I don't want to live with you. I—I want us to stop seeing each other.' John stared at her in disbelief.

'What on earth do you mean? Stop seeing

17

each other? Why? What have I done? What's happened?'

Patsy clenched her hands together and tried to keep her voice from shaking.

'You haven't done anything, John,' she said as steadily as she could. 'You have always been very good to me. You are too good to me. It's just that I've suddenly realised that I don't want to marry you. I don't love you enough.'

'Patsy, you can't mean it.' His expression was incredulous. 'What on earth has made you suddenly decide this?'

'I don't think it's really suddenly,' she said slowly. 'I think I've been feeling like it for a long time but just went on drifting along.'

'You mean you're just throwing me over. Just like that, with no reason?'

'But there is a reason, John. I just told you.'

He shook his head slightly. 'I just can't believe it, Pats. Hadn't you better think about it a bit more? We're so right for each other, you know we are.'

Patsy shook her head and burst into desperate speech. 'I like you very much,' she said, 'and I thought I loved you, but I've realised that I don't want to spend the rest of my life with you. It's been very wrong of me but I've just drifted into a relationship with you and I know now that it's not strong enough to lead to marriage. You deserve someone who will love you whole-heartedly, and I've been wrong to let it go on for so long. I should have realised sooner. I—'

'Is there someone else?' John broke in, and Patsy shook her head.

'No. There's no-one else,' she said. 'I just feel that I'm in a rut and I must get out of it. John—c-couldn't we go on being friends and just see each other occasionally.'

He jumped to his feet with anger taking the place of bewilderment on his face.

'Go on being friends!' he echoed her words. 'No, we couldn't! You tell me that you're tired of me. That after all this time you don't after all want to marry me thank you very much, but you'd like me still around, like a little dog or something, just there in case you want me. Well, you can't have it both ways, so you'd better make up your mind.'

Patsy's face whitened, but she realised that his anger came from hurt and surprise, and she went on as calmly as she could.

'I have made up my mind, John,' she said quietly. 'As soon as I knew that I couldn't marry you I told you. I do like you very much indeed, but that's not enough for marriage, and to be fair to you—'

'Fair!' he broke in again. 'Do you think it's fair to keep me hanging about all this time and then suddenly out of the blue tell me that you don't want to marry me?'

'I'm sorry,' she repeated helplessly. 'I really am sorry, John. Please don't think too badly of me. If we are going to part let's do it without anger. We've had some very happy times together, and—'

'And you'd like to keep me still on tap for future occasions,' he said bitterly. Patsy looked up at him with tears in her brown eyes, and his voice changed. 'This is just a phase you're going through Pats,' he said softly. 'We don't need to rush into marriage. Let's leave it a bit and you'll change your mind again.'

Patsy's tears threatened to overflow at the sudden softening of his voice, but she replied resolutely.

'No, John, I won't change my mind, but I wish that we could go on being friends. Perhaps we could still play tennis together sometimes?'

'No thanks!' the hard look was back on his face. 'I was never one to stay where I'm not wanted,' he declared. 'I'll go; and I just hope you don't regret it!' Without another word or a backward look he turned on his heel and left. Patsy sat still with tears at last running down her cheeks as she heard his car start and its sound receded into the distance. She felt as if she would never be able to move again, but at last she brushed the tears from her cheeks and mechanically carried the now-cold coffee through to the kitchen. She felt battered and tired, and very sorry that she had obviously hurt John so much, but not regretful. 'I had to do it,' she thought. 'Perhaps his pride is hurt more than his heart. I hope so, he'd get over that quicker; but in any case he's so attractive and so nice, he'll soon find another girl, and I hope he'll be as happy as he deserves to be.' She sat for a while in the tiny sitting-room, staring into space. 'And what about me?' she thought. 'What shall I do? Will I find someone else too? I expect I'll be very lonely for a time. I've been out of touch with everyone except John. I wish I could go away, make a fresh start somewhere.' As this thought entered her head she suddenly sat up straighter.

'There's nothing to stop me doing just that,' she thought. 'There's no need for me to stay on in Lynn even. I could get another job somewhere else. I could even have a holiday and explore a bit before I try to get another job. I have never even used any of the income from the sale of the house, so I could easily afford it.' Slightly cheered by these ideas she went to bed, where to her surprise she fell at once into a deep, dreamless sleep.

When she awoke the next morning her first thought was of John and she probed her feeling gently like someone touching an aching tooth. She found that her chief sense was one of relief. 'I've done it,' she thought. 'I'm sure John will soon recover, and I am going to make a fresh start.' Sue boarded the bus at a stop much nearer the school and they walked in together as they usually did, to arrive about half an hour before the first of the children. 'How was your evening?' she asked Sue, and the other girl rolled her eyes and shrugged.

'Well it started off all right,' she answered, 'but we had the usual row about where to go after the flicks. I wanted to go dancing and Pete said he was too tired. He can be a real drag sometimes.' Patsy laughed.

'Oh, you two,' she said. 'You're always quarrelling.'

'It's what makes us get on so well together,' Sue declared paradoxically. 'We both always say what we think and so we know where we are.'

'Yes,' Patsy said slowly. 'That is a good thing.'

'Do you and your John never quarrel?' Sue asked curiously.

'He isn't "*my* John" any more,' Patsy told her steadily.

'What? You *have* quarrelled, then?'

'No. We haven't quarrelled. I just realised that I don't love him enough and I don't want to marry him.'

'Well!' Sue was obviously astonished. 'You two always behaved as if you were married already,' she said. 'What on earth got into you?'

'Perhaps that was it,' Patsy tried to explain. 'We just drifted along.' Sue shook her head.

'Well,' she said, accepting the fact but not understanding it. 'We'll have to arrange some double dates. You've been out of circulation for so long, hardly anybody knows you exist any more.'

Patsy smiled. 'Thanks, but no thanks,' she said. 'I've got other plans. I'm going to resign from the job and take a little break before I get another.'

'Well, well! You're certainly full of surprises this morning. Are you really sure about all this?'

'Yes, I'm sure. I'm very happy in this job, but it isn't everything, and as you say, I'm really out of touch. I just drifted into a relationship with John, which was very unfair to him, and I've decided that I won't go on drifting any longer. I'll take a holiday and try to sort myself out, and then I'll take another job, maybe in another town.'

'Wow! You certainly are burning your boats, aren't you. Are you quite sure, Patsy?'

'Yes, I'm quite sure. I'll give a month's notice today. They'll easily find someone for next term, and between now and then I'll decide exactly where I'm going to go.'

'I'll miss you,' Sue declared. 'We've always worked so well together.'

'So you will with the next teacher,' Patsy told her. 'You're very easy to get on with.'

'Pete doesn't think so,' Sue grinned, 'but I guess he loves me just the way I am.'

Mrs Crossley, the school supervisor, accepted Patsy's resignation with regret. 'Of course we'll have no difficulty in replacing you,' she said. 'There are more teachers than

23

there are jobs. But I'm very sorry that you want to go. Would you like to think about it for a bit longer? Are you sure you won't change your mind?'

'I am quite sure, thank you,' Patsy assured her. 'I have very much enjoyed the job, but I am definitely sure that I need a change.'

'Well, I will of course give you an excellent testimonial, or you may refer any future prospective employer to me.' Patsy thanked her, and then on chance called at the solicitor's office to see if he was free. His secretary told her that he was at that moment with a client but that if she cared to wait Mr Phelps would be free for the rest of the afternoon. 'Not that there's much of the afternoon left,' she added with a smile.

'I won't keep him long,' Patsy promised. 'It's just a matter of courtesy really. I want to tell him of my future plans.'

Unlike Mrs Crossley, Mr Phelps was delighted at what Patsy had to tell him. 'You've never even had a proper holiday since your mother died,' he said. 'In every school holiday you've just mooned about here. It's time you saw a bit more of the world. You're only young once, you know.' Patsy smiled at his enthusiasm. 'How long are you going to take off, and where are you going?' he wanted to know.

'I haven't thought that far yet,' she told him. 'I've got at least a month in which to make up

24

my mind.'

'Well, let me know when you do; and be sure to come to me if you need any help or advice.'

'I will,' Patsy promised him, and went home feeling content that she had taken the first decisive steps towards her future.

Over the next few weeks Patsy made and cast aside many plans, but in the meantime she made steady preparations for what she thought of as her new life. Jan and Peter were also sorry to see her go. They knew they would have no trouble in letting the flat, and could even be choosy about who they would take, but there was no guarantee that they would get as good a tenant as Patsy had been. She sold them her car. At first she had toyed with the idea of just driving off and staying where she fancied, but she decided that for a while she would like to have no responsibilities, not even that of a car. She had very few possessions; she had removed only a few things from her mother's house, and she arranged for these to be collected and stored. She haunted travel agents, collecting brochures and studying them avidly. She didn't want a package tour, she decided. For one thing they were too short, she wanted to stay away for much longer than two or three weeks. She would try to find somewhere abroad to live for a month or two, she thought, so that she could travel around locally a bit and get to know something of whichever country she chose. The difficulty was which country to choose. Somewhere warm, she thought, perhaps somewhere where she had to learn another language to get along. These thoughts stimulated her, and she felt grateful that she had enough money to make such plans and carry them out. She talked again with Mr Phelps and he entered whole-heartedly into her tentative plans.

'Don't go anywhere too wild,' he advised. 'I mean don't go rushing off to the wilds of Africa or somewhere like that.' Smilingly she assured him that she wouldn't. 'And let me arrange for money to come to you regularly wherever you go.'

'I feel as if wherever I go I'll be safe with you behind me,' she told him.

'Well, I might easily have been your father,' he surprised her by saying. 'I thought I was doing quite well with your mother until your father turned up.'

'I always thought you were *his* friend.'

'Oh, I was, afterwards, but it was through your mother that I got to know him.'

The term ended and with it Patsy's job. With Sue as an eager and enthusiastic adviser, Patsy had an orgy of shopping. 'I haven't decided exactly where I'm going,' she told her slightly envious friend, 'but I'm going to choose somewhere warm, so all I want to buy are summer clothes.'

'You're going to have to make up your mind

soon or else find somewhere else to live. Your flat will be occupied by someone else in less than two weeks' time.'

Patsy agreed and gave more attention than ever to the many brightly-coloured brochures that littered the tiny flat she was so soon to leave; and then fate took a hand and all her tentative plans were abandoned and she had decided where she would go.

CHAPTER THREE

It was Monday morning and Patsy was on her way to the travel agents. At last she had made up her mind. She was going to Australia. She could go, she had found out, on a tour for four weeks, flying to Sydney and staying there for a while, and then moving on for a week at a time to other places of interest. 'Supposing I don't want to stay with the party?' she had asked the very helpful girl with whom she had spoken.

'No problem at all,' the girl assured her. 'In fact lots of people don't. It works out to be a fairly cheap way to go there, and some people who have relatives or friends there spend some of the time with them.'

'And supposing I don't want to come back when everyone else does?'

'Again no problem, as long as you realise that your ticket can't be transferred to another flight. If you want to come back later than everyone else you will have to make other arrangements, and that of course will make the whole thing more expensive.' Patsy had thanked her and said she would think it over. She had done so and she had also talked to kindly Mr Phelps about it. 'It seems rather a long way to go just to have a change,' he had said, 'but why not? You can afford it, and now is the time to do what you want to do. Take as

28

much money as you are allowed to take, and let me know as far in advance as you can if you decide that you do want to stay on for a while.' So now Patsy was on her way to book her flight. This particular trip left on Friday, but the girl had assured her that there were still one or two seats available.

The day was sunny but chilly and Patsy found herself looking forward to blue skies and warm days. There was a spring in her step as she walked. At first she had felt apprehensive and somehow vulnerable walking through the streets. She had imagined all the time that she would suddenly come face to face with John, and she wondered what they would say or do; but she had never seen him, not even in the distance, since the night he had stalked out of her flat, and although they had always spent so much time together, she was amazed at how little she missed him. Of course she had been very busy, but even so it had been in many ways a relief to think only of what she would like to do, and not to have to think what would please John. She glanced idly into shop windows as she passed them, but all her shopping was done, and there was nothing else that she wanted to buy. She had even let her supplies at home run low and on one or two evenings had eaten her solitary dinner in a small restaurant. 'I could take off tomorrow if I wanted to,' she thought exultantly. As she walked along in this happy

29

frame of mind, her attention was attracted to a man and a small child who stood together in front of a toy-shop window. There was something about the man that looked slightly foreign, she thought. Perhaps it was just his clothes, which seemed different in a way that she could not readily define; but it was the little girl who really attracted her attention.

She stood like a little statue, seeming entirely disinterested in the contents of the window, or what the man was saying to her. Curiously, Patsy lingered to listen. 'Do you like the dolls, poppet?' he asked. There was no answer from the tiny figure by his side, and he crouched down beside her. 'What do you say, Tanya, shall we go inside and have a look at everything? We'll buy anything that you would like.' The little figure didn't move or speak, and before Patsy had time to speculate any more, it happened. The pavement was fairly clear and along it came a boy of about nine on a skateboard. He was obviously new to it and had not much control, and as he tried to lean to one side and steer his way past them he slipped and fell off. He fell right on to the crouched figure of the man and the little girl, knocking them both over, and his skateboard went on down the pavement and shot out into the road. A bicycle passing by wavered dangerously, and a car swerved involuntarily to miss it. Ignoring the boy, whose knee was bleeding slightly, Patsy bent to pick up the little girl while her companion rolled over and scrambled to his feet. 'Are you hurt?' she asked as she lifted the child. There was no answer, but to her surprise the little girl took one look at her and then clasped her arms tightly around Patsy's neck and clung to her as if she would never let go. The boy had risen shakily to his feet as well, and looked rather white-faced. 'I'm sorry, mister,' he said breathlessly. 'I didn't mean to do it.'

'Is she all right?' the man asked Patsy.

'I think so,' she answered, and he turned his attention to the boy. 'Surely you know you shouldn't take that thing on the pavement where people are?' he demanded angrily.

'Yes, sir. I'm sorry. I didn't think. My mum'll kill me if I'm in trouble with it.' A few passers-by had stopped to watch and listen, and some to give their opinions.

'Shouldn't be allowed at all,' one woman said. 'On the pavement or off it.'

'Need a good hiding, you do,' an elderly man told the boy. 'We weren't allowed to go about being a danger to other people when I was a boy.' The man, who was now holding on to the boy's arm, shook it slightly.

'Go carefully and get that contraption and carry it home,' he said, 'and don't use it in the street any more.'

'No, sir. Thank you, sir. I won't,' said the boy, obviously relieved to get off so lightly.

'Shouldn't just let him go like that,' the

woman said, but he ignored her and turned to Patsy.

'He's had a fright,' he remarked, 'and I should think he'll keep off the pavements after this. Thank you for picking her up. The boy didn't hurt you, did he?'

'No, I'm perfectly all right,' she assured him. He put out his arms to take the child. 'Come, Tanya,' he said, but the little arms tightened around Patsy's neck, and the little face was buried in her shoulder.

'I'm sorry,' he said, briefly dusting his trousers and again attempting to take the child. 'I guess she'd had a bit of a shock. Poor little devil. That's the last thing she needed on top of everything else.' Patsy stood silent, not knowing what to say. Still holding the child she took stock of the tall figure in front of her. He looked about thirty, she thought, and he had jet-black hair and the bluest eyes she had ever seen. His face was brown, and his nose ever so slightly hooked, over a firm mouth. A very powerful-looking face, she thought, a bit like a pirate. He looked at her face above the child's curly head. Dark curls mingled with the child's fair ones, and brown eyes looked at him gravely. 'Look,' he said suddenly, 'if you don't mind hanging on to her a bit longer, let's go and have a cup of coffee somewhere.'

'It doesn't look as if I have much choice,' Patsy smiled. 'There's a coffee-shop just across the road.'

'Can you carry her that far? I don't know why she's behaving like this, but I can explain a little.'

'I can manage,' Patsy told him. 'It's not very far.' And with his hand under her elbow, half supporting the child, they crossed the road.

'I don't really know how much I can say in front of her,' he said when they had settled at a table and he had ordered coffee. 'She's my brother's child, and I've come to take her back with me to Sri Lanka.'

'That explains his different look,' Patsy thought. 'It's the suit. It's made of very lightweight material, not at all like an English suit.'

'There—there was an accident,' he said, and Patsy saw pain in his eyes. 'Both were killed. He at once, and she later, in hospital.'

'I'm sorry,' Patsy murmured, quite shaken by these sudden confidences.

'They were a very close family,' he went on, 'and although she,' he nodded his head slightly towards the child, 'was only bruised, she hasn't spoken at all since it happened. The doctors say that it is extreme shock, and that only time will help.' The child still clung to Patsy and Patsy moved her a little into a more comfortable position.

'I feel so helpless,' he said almost angrily. 'He was my only brother. Jenny, his wife, was an only child too and an orphan. From the time the child was born it was legally arranged that I should be her guardian if anything happened to them. Of course we never dreamed that it would, but Rory adored his wife and child and wanted every eventuality taken care of.'

'When—' Patsy began hesitantly, and he answered her unspoken question.

'Only four days ago,' he said. 'I came at once.'

There was a little silence as the waitress brought their coffee. Then he said, 'She's been taken care of at the children's home since then, but she doesn't really seem to know or care where she is or what is happening. This clinging to you is the first sign of any emotion that she has given.'

He looked at her intently. 'You are very like Jenny,' he said speculatively. 'I wonder if that could be it.'

Patsy bent her head over the child. 'Would you like a drink of milk, or lemonade?' she asked, but there was no reply.

'I should have introduced myself,' the man said suddenly. 'I'm sorry. My name is Gavin. Gavin O'Rourke, and this is Tanya.'

'Hallo, Tanya,' Patsy said softly, and then, 'My name is Patsy Marley, and—well— perhaps I'd better come with you to take her back. It would be easier, wouldn't it?'

'I'd be very grateful. I don't really want to drag a protesting child from your arms. I just hope she'll consent to let you go when we get

34

there. I wonder if I ought to get the doctor to have a look at her.'

'I shouldn't think that's necessary,' Patsy reassured him. 'She's not even scratched, just startled a little.' They finished their coffee in silence, and then Gavin glanced at his watch.

'I hope I'm not keeping you from anything?' he asked. 'It's very kind of you to come with me.' He smiled ruefully. 'I really do need some help.'

'What are you going to do?' Patsy asked.

'Well, the doctor says that there is no reason why I shouldn't take her back with me straightaway. In fact it might even be better for her. I haven't booked a flight yet. In fact I was hoping to do so this morning, but I think the best thing to do now is to take her back and then come out again by myself. If you've finished I'll see if I can use the phone to get us a taxi.'

Patsy had often walked past the children's home but she had never been inside, and she looked around with interest. The girl who received them looked to be about twenty-five, and she hurried forward with a questioning look. 'Is anything wrong?' she asked. Gavin quickly explained, and the girl led them into a tiny sitting-room.

'I don't think she's hurt at all,' Gavin went on, 'but I can't get her away from Miss Marley. I can only think it's the similarity—' His voice trailed away.

'Come along, Tanya,' the girl said coaxingly. 'Come and have some lunch. Miss Marley has to go now.' The child gave no sign of having heard, and after a few minutes silence Patsy bent her head and said softly:

'Tanya, I do have to go now, but if you go and have your lunch I promise I'll come and see you afterwards.'

The little girl did not answer but her arms loosened slightly, and Patsy followed up this advantage. 'I'm just going to do a little shopping while you eat your lunch and then you can watch for me from the window.' Gently she disentangled the little arms and set the child on her feet. 'Off you go,' she said. 'I'll come back soon, I promise.'

The girl took Tanya's hand and led her from the room. She looked back at the doorway and Patsy waved to her. 'I'll see you again soon,' she said. Gavin ran his hand through his hair.

'I am sorry,' he said. 'Here you are out minding your own business, and with probably a thousand things to do, and you get mixed up in all this.'

'It's all right,' Patsy told him. 'Whatever I was going to do I can do later.'

'Well will you come and have lunch with me? And did you really mean that you would come back and see the child?'

'Of course I did. For some reason, what she seems to want right now is me, and if I can give her any comfort at all—'

Gavin reached across and briefly touched her hand, and Patsy's heart beat a little faster. What a dynamic man he was. Everything about him seemed larger than life. 'Will you lunch with me?' he asked again. 'And if you will, where is a good place to go?'

'I'd love to,' she told him simply, 'and I think the Red Lion is very good, and it's not very far away; we can easily walk there, and get back soon to see Tanya.'

They were soon seated in the dining-room of the hotel, and Gavin kept up a flow of small-talk until they had ordered and been served.

'Here's to you!' he toasted her with the first glass of wine. 'A real ministering angel.' Patsy felt herself blushing.

'I'm glad I was able to help,' she said, 'even though it was only momentarily. What are you going to do now.' He ran his hand through his unruly black hair in the gesture that she remembered from earlier.

'What I'd like to do is crawl into bed and sleep for a couple of days,' he said with a tired smile. 'I haven't had much sleep in the last five days, but with so much to think about and Tanya to worry about, I guess I wouldn't find it easy to sleep anyhow.'

'Poor baby,' Patsy murmured. 'Her whole world has been turned upside down.'

'Anyhow, enough of my troubles,' Gavin smiled. 'Tell me about yourself. Where were you off to when we ruined your day?'

'Well actually, I was on my way to book a flight to Australia.' She laughed a little at his surprise.

'Australia? Well, that's a surprise. When are you going, and why? That is, if you don't mind telling me. Somehow I feel as if I've known you for a long time.'

Patsy took a sip of her wine. 'Of course I don't mind telling you,' she said, picking up her fork again. 'There's nothing secret about it.' Briefly she told him of all that had led up to her decision to go away for a while, and how long it had taken her to make up her mind where to go. 'Did you enjoy working in the nursery school?' he asked.

'I loved it, and I expect I shall come back to a similar job. I'm very fond of children.'

'You're certainly very good with them. I should imagine one needs a lot of patience. I'm afraid that children are a closed book to me. I hadn't time to make any real plans, and I ought to get back as soon as I can; there are several business deals pending that need my presence.'

'What *is* your business?' Patsy asked curiously.

'Tea,' he answered briefly. 'I've got a couple of large tea plantations, and I also deal personally with the export side of it. For that I have an office in Colombo, and I live just outside. The plantations are slightly to the south. It's a good life, suits me fine. I enjoy what I do, too.' He paused for a moment and then went on, 'Of course I shall have to change my way of life a bit now that I've become a surrogate father.'

'Are you married?' Patsy asked, thinking briefly of the mother Tanya had also lost.

'No, not yet,' he answered. 'There is someone, but I don't quite know what she'll feel about a ready-made family. We hadn't time to discuss it before I left.' Patsy gazed at him in surprise.

'But surely—' she began, and then stopped. 'I'm sorry, of course it's no business of mine.'

'Don't apologise. I can probably guess what you were going to say; but you know, Patsy, not every woman feels the way you do about children.'

'What's going to happen to Tanya when you get back?'

'Well, the doctors have assured me that this silence of hers is a temporary thing caused by shock, and that there is no reason why I can't take her back straightaway; in fact they seem to think it might be the best thing to take her right away as soon as possible. I have a very good housekeeper, and I thought that when I got back I would engage someone to look after Tanya, but I see now that it's not going to be easy to find the right person. She's obviously going to need a lot of loving care and endless patience. I'll give her as much time as I can,

39

but she'll need someone more constant than that in her life.' He smiled ruefully. 'I'm going to have to learn fast about children.'

'I wonder why she decided that she would cling to me?' Patsy wondered aloud.

'Well, as I said, you do look very like her mother, but it can't have been just that. There was evidently something about you right from the moment you picked her up that she felt she could trust.'

'Poor baby,' Patsy repeated. 'I wish I could help more.'

Gavin suddenly put down his knife and fork and looked at her intently. As she felt the intensity of his look Patsy sat very still. She knew what he was thinking, and the same thought had instantly come to her.

'Patsy, could you—would you?'

'Come back with you, you mean?'

'Yes. Oh I know I've no right to ask it, but such a lot is at stake for that infant, and you did say that you weren't at all sure where you wanted to go. Of course it wouldn't be the holiday you were planning, but I'd make it as pleasant as I could for you, and—'

'I didn't so much want a holiday as a change,' Patsy interrupted, 'and I'm so used to having my time fully occupied that I think I would probably very soon get bored with having nothing to do.' They stared at each other across the table, food forgotten.

'You don't know anything about me except

40

what I've told you,' Gavin reminded her, 'but my brother's solicitor will vouch for me.'

'I would have to go and see Mr Phelps, my solicitor, too,' she told him. 'He's been so kind and helpful to me, and I promised to let him know where I was going and when. As a matter of fact I was going to pop in to see him this afternoon after I'd booked my flight. Perhaps he could get together with your man, and—'

'Oh Patsy, I'll never be able to thank you enough! I've been at my wits' end for the last two days. You're like the answer to a prayer.'

Patsy pushed back her chair. 'I don't want any more to eat,' she declared. 'Let's go and collect Tanya, and start doing all the things we have to do.'

CHAPTER FOUR

Tanya greeted them with silent intensity, and Gavin had a brief word with the matron in charge, and told her that he would keep the child out until bedtime, and that he was going to get a flight for them as soon as possible. Patsy had phoned Mr Phelps before they left the hotel and at the urgency in her voice he had agreed that she could come to see him almost at once. If he was surprised to see her walk in with a strange man and a child he didn't show it. Under the calm gaze of the old man she explained all that had happened since she set out that morning, which now seemed a lifetime ago. Gavin sat silently until she had finished. 'Of course neither of you know anything about me,' he said then, 'but I hoped that you would get in touch with my brother's solicitor, who can vouch for me. He's been our family solicitor for years and—'

'I hardly think an orphan child would be used as an incentive to white slavery,' Mr Phelps interrupted drily. 'What is the name of your solicitor?'

'It's Barney and Goodchild, Mr Peterson is the actual solicitor.'

'Ah! Old Peterson. I know him well. We're contemporaries. Play golf together; occasionally cross each other in court. I'll get together with him. I suppose you want a contract drawn up?' Neither of them had thought of it.

'Whatever you think best, sir,' Gavin told him. 'May we leave everything to you? I want the best possible deal for Patsy. She'll be doing me such a great service.'

'Salary?' the old man asked.

'I've no idea,' Gavin admitted. 'Please make it very generous, I'm a rich man; and please also see that all Patsy's interests are covered for any situation that may arise.'

The solicitor looked from one to the other, and then at the child on Patsy's knee. 'When do you want all this?' he asked.

'As soon as possible please, Mr Phelps,' Patsy answered. 'There's nothing else to wait for. We wanted to book a flight this afternoon.'

'Hurry, hurry,' he grumbled gently but with a smile in his eyes. 'All right. I'll contact Peterson today and you can come in again the day after tomorrow.'

'Thank you very much, sir.' Gavin stretched out his hand. 'I'm very much obliged to you.' The older man took his hand, and then shook Patsy's. 'I'm glad you've found something to do, child,' he said. 'I don't think a long holiday was what you really needed.'

From the solicitor's office they went straight to the travel agent and there Gavin got tickets for the Thursday flight. 'What do you need to buy before we go?' he asked, and Patsy smiled

43

up at him.

'Nothing,' she answered. 'I've already done all my shopping; but Tanya will need clothes. I don't expect that she has anything suitable for a hot climate. I expect you have things to do. Would you like me to take her shopping?'

'I'd be immensely grateful. I drew out a sizeable amount of cash this morning, so please will you get her everything you think she needs, and also anything that happens to take her fancy.'

'I'll keep her with me until it's time for her to go back,' Patsy said.

'Bless you; and I'll meet you there and we can have dinner together.' He bent to kiss the unresponsive child. 'B'Bye, Tanya. Patsy's going to take you shopping and I'll see you later,' he said.

'What does she call you?' Patsy asked as he turned to go.

'Well, so far this trip she hasn't called me anything, but it was Uncle Gavin when I came over last year. I don't know if she even remembers me though. She was only three then.'

The whole afternoon was spent in shopping. Patsy thought it would be better to get everything at once, and also that it would be no bad thing for the child to become thoroughly tired before she was taken back and left. Throughout the afternoon she chatted steadily about what they were buying, and tried gently to get the child to show some preference for colour. Tanya submitted to being measured, and to trying on shoes and dresses, but uttered no word. When they had finished and were laden with parcels, she went to a nearby bookshop and bought several bright picture-books. 'I think we'd better get a taxi home,' she decided, and asked the bookstore assistant to call one for her. Jan and Peter were gardening when the taxi drew up and they looked in surprise when they saw the child and the many parcels. 'This is Tanya,' Patsy said. 'Oh there's such a lot to tell you, but I can't do it now.'

They smiled at the child and tried to conceal their curiosity. Her silence they mistook for shyness. 'Make it soon,' Jan urged. 'Did you buy your ticket?'

'No. My plans have all changed,' Patsy laughed. 'You'll never believe it all. Can I come in later tonight and tell you?'

'You'd better!' Peter told her. 'We're dying to know.'

Upstairs, Patsy made tea for herself, and gave Tanya some milk and biscuits. Then together they looked at the picture-books, with Patsy keeping up a steady monologue about what was in them. At seven o'clock she phoned for a taxi, and leaving everything but the books behind, they went back to the children's home. As they arrived, Tanya's hand closed more tightly on hers and Patsy returned the pressure reassuringly. 'Uncle Gavin will be here to say goodnight to you,' she said, 'and tomorrow I'll come for you as soon as you've had your breakfast.' Gavin was already there and they sat and chatted for a little time before the same girl came to take the child away to bed. For a moment she clung fiercely to Patsy, and Patsy reiterated her promise to return the next morning. Reluctantly Tanya let the girl lead her away, and she clung tightly to her picture-books.

'Did you do all you wanted to do?' Patsy asked Gavin as they walked down the short driveway.

'I'm ashamed to say that I did nothing but sleep,' he told her. 'I thought I'd just lie down for a little while and the next thing I knew, it was six o'clock.'

'I expect it did you good. We got everything that Tanya needs, but I'm afraid I haven't much change for you.'

'You must be feeling tired now,' he suggested, 'but not too tired to have dinner with me, I hope. Let's go somewhere and have a quiet drink first.'

Sitting in the dim light of a nearby hotel bar, Patsy realised that she was indeed tired. 'What a lot has happened since I left home this morning,' she mused.

'Nothing but good has happened to me,' he told her. 'I hope it will turn out to be like that for you too.'

'It's all very exciting,' she confided. 'Mr Phelps was right, I didn't really want a holiday, just a change, and this is going to be a complete change.'

'Do you have much to do before we leave?' he asked.

'Hardly anything. I was all prepared to leave anyway.'

'Then perhaps the three of us could spend the next few days in getting to know each other better,' he suggested.

'I'd like that,' Patsy admitted. 'I think it would be good for Tanya too.'

'Shall I meet you in the morning at about nine?' he suggested, and Patsy nodded her agreement.

They moved through to the dining-room and ordered a meal, taking their drinks with them. They talked little and there were long companionable silences. 'I hope you're not having any regrets?' Gavin said once, and Patsy shook her head.

'I just can't believe my luck,' he went on. 'Mine and Tanya's. Patsy—if you do have any regrets or second thoughts about what you're doing, you must tell me. It's all been so sudden.'

'I won't,' she assured him. 'I feel that I've been lucky too.'

'I'll take you home,' he said, as they sipped their coffee. 'It's early, but you've had an exhausting day.'

When the taxi stopped at her gate she invited him in, but he declined with a smile. 'You have an early night,' he suggested, 'and think it all over and find out if you're really sure that you want to come.'

As the taxi left, Patsy went towards the door, and was pounced upon at once by Jan and Peter.

'We're dying of curiosity!' Jan said. 'Come in and have a drink and tell us what you've been up to all day.'

They listened avidly as Patsy recounted all that had happened since she'd left home that morning. 'How lucky for everybody,' Jan remarked. 'That you really wanted a job and a change of place, and they so badly needed you.'

'I hope you're not acting too hastily,' Peter said gravely. 'It's a big step to take so suddenly.'

'I wouldn't feel any different about it if I thought it over for weeks,' Patsy told him, 'and for some reason or other Tanya really needs me.'

The next two days Gavin, Patsy and Tanya spent exclusively in each other's company. 'I think you have the right idea about keeping her fully occupied,' Gavin told Patsy, 'so we'll fill these days as full as we can. I've hired a car, so we can be as mobile as we want to be.'

'We could spend a day at the zoo,' Patsy suggested, and so they did. Tanya did not speak, but she was not quite so clinging now that she realised that Patsy was going to stay with her. The adults ignored her silence and pointed out to her various things of interest, and bought her peanuts with which to feed the monkeys. They stayed the whole day and the child fell asleep sprawled across Patsy's lap as they drove back to Lynn. On the second day, again at Patsy's suggestion, they drove to the coast and walked along the deserted spring beach. It was a lovely day and they found a sheltered spot to sit. Gavin left them there and went off in search of shops to buy Tanya a spade and pail. She accepted them quietly but with obvious pleasure and she and Gavin constructed castles of sand while Patsy found shells with which to decorate them.

Thursday seemed to come very quickly, and Patsy felt a little thrill of excitement when she awoke. They had bought two extra suitcases, and all of Tanya's new clothes were packed. They had not told her about the journey, thinking that it would be better to tell her when they hadn't got to leave her for another night. Gavin was going to pick her up and come out to Patsy at lunchtime. 'You must have one last morning to yourself,' he had insisted. 'We've monopolised you ever since we found you.' Now she stretched deliciously in bed, thought of the packed suitcases with all the new clothes, the long journey to come and the new life ahead. The more she saw of Gavin the more she liked him, and already Tanya had a special place in her heart.

The day seemed to pass in a flash. The flight was at six and so, soon after lunch, it was time to set out for the airport. Patsy had explained to Tanya, 'We're going on a long journey, darling, in a car and in an aeroplane, and then in another car; and then we're both going to live with Uncle Gavin.' Tanya had looked at her solemnly and then turned and put her little hand into Gavin's. A big smile lit up his face as he gently squeezed it. The airport was full of noise and bustle and there was the inevitable waiting about, but at last they were airborne, and Patsy felt that her new life had really begun.

It was a long flight and they were all glad when it was over. Tanya had slept for most of the night and when they disembarked briefly at Rome, and then Bahrain, she had unprotestingly let Gavin carry her. When the plane at last touched down at Colombo, Gavin gave a sigh of relief. 'It's good to be here,' he declared. 'I expect there'll be someone to meet us. I telexed the time of our arrival.' Customs and other formalities were soon over, and as they walked towards the exit, a porter following with their luggage, Patsy saw a tall, slim, blonde girl waving, and Gavin confirmed her guess.

'It's Elaine,' he said, and quickened his step a little.

'Darling!' The girl flung her arms around Gavin's neck. 'It's been ages! I would so much rather have come with you, but I've held the fort nobly, and you have no problems to come back to.'

Gavin held her briefly and then swung her round to face the other two. 'This is Tanya,' he said, 'and Patsy, who is going to look after her.' The tall slim girl looked from Patsy to the child as he went on, 'Patsy, this is Elaine, who's been in charge while I've been away, and who as you just heard has kept everything ticking over.' Patsy extended her hand and Elaine took it briefly, before she turned again to Gavin and said:

'Well, what a surprise. You must have worked fast. You didn't say you were bringing back a nanny. I've been looking around for a Singhalese nanny.'

'Patsy is not exactly a nanny,' Gavin said. 'She's more in the nature of a guardian angel; but I'll explain it all to you later. Right now what we three want is a shower, a change of clothes and a long cold drink.'

The drive from the airport took about half an hour and Patsy was entranced by all she saw. Colombo itself seemed full of noise and colour. Car horns hooted continually, and the women in their brightly-coloured saris looked like little groups of exotic birds. When they left the city there were different things to see. Patsy pointed out two oxen-drawn carts, and

51

Tanya's eyes grew round as she saw rickshaws bowling along. Soon they were driving through what looked like a prosperous collection of houses. There were beautifully manicured lawns, and a riot of exotic flowers; sprinklers seemed to be in every garden and the bright drops of water flashed like jewels in the sunshine. There was a sprinkler going in Gavin's garden too, and as the car drove in through the gates and up the gravelled drive, Patsy thought in what pleasant surroundings she was about to live.

CHAPTER FIVE

Her first impressions were confirmed in the days that followed. The house was low and big, with high-ceilinged rooms and large windows. She was introduced to Mrs Jancsz, the plump, friendly and competent housekeeper, and to three quiet-footed servants whose names she had difficulty at first in remembering. They were very unobtrusive, but the house always looked immaculate, and excellent meals appeared regularly. Patsy soon found that all she had to do was be a companion to Tanya, and she was happy to devote all her time to the child. Gavin always had breakfast with them and then disappeared for the rest of the day, but he made a point of being home so that he could spend some time with them before Tanya went to bed. At the first weekend he took them together with Elaine to the country club, of which he was a member, and where, he told Patsy, they could swim, have lunch or do whatever else they wanted. 'I don't want you to be just shut away with the child all the time,' he said. 'Of course you will gradually meet all my friends, but you'll also probably meet people here. There's a car, and I've told the driver to be available whenever you want him. Later on, when you know your way around a bit, you may prefer to drive yourself.' They discovered that Tanya had absolutely no fear of the water, and could even swim a few strokes. Gavin spent about an hour with her in the shallow end of the pool, while Patsy and Elaine lay side by side on long chairs without speaking. The presence of the other girl was the only thing that prevented Patsy's complete enjoyment of these first days in Sri Lanka. She had dined with them often, and Patsy imagined that it was a standing habit, except perhaps when they went out somewhere. She would arrive beautifully groomed and dressed soon after Tanya had gone to bed, and in spite of her new wardrobe, Patsy always felt like a country mouse beside her. She was always quite polite, but she rarely included Patsy directly in the conversation, and often chatted about things and people about which Patsy knew nothing.

Any feelings of inadequacy were dispelled however when Tanya began at last to speak. Patsy had bought her some large, coloured magic markers, and several drawing-books, and during the hot afternoons when they both rested they would amuse themselves with these. One afternoon Patsy drew a picture of an aeroplane, and showed it to Tanya, saying, 'Aeroplane. Now it's your turn.' They had played this game several times before and the child had always silently proffered her drawings and Patsy had commented on them. This time she found herself looking at a crude drawing of a man with very long legs and lots of black hair. 'A man,' she said, 'with a red shirt and—' At first she thought she had imagined it, but when she leaned closer she heard Tanya repeat softly, 'Uncle Gavin'. Patsy wanted to grab the child and hug her, but she forced herself to reply calmly.

'So it is. Can you draw yourself and me with him?' The curly head bent again over the paper, and after a few minutes it was held out for Patsy's inspection. 'Tanya,' she said, pointing to the smaller figure, 'and'—She let her voice rise as if in question and to her delight Tanya pointed and murmured, 'Patsy.'

She did not press any more but she was in a fever of impatience for Gavin to come home to hear of this miracle. When at last he came in she went quickly to the doorway to meet him and grasped his arm tightly.

'What is it?' he asked, looking down at her in concern. 'Is anything wrong?'

She shook her head ever so slightly, and then said in a louder than usual voice, 'Hallo, Gavin. It's nice to see you back.' Squeezing his arm she added, 'Tanya, say hallo to Uncle Gavin.'

Before he fully grasped what she had said, the little girl came over to them both and murmured shyly, 'Hallo, Uncle Gavin.' Patsy's grip on his arm was renewed.

'I want to sing and shout,' she whispered, 'but I think it would be best not to make a

55

fuss.'

He put his free arm around her shoulders. 'Well, I've just got to hug somebody so it had better be you!' he declared, and pulled her to him in a bear-like hug. Tanya smiled at them, and he released Patsy and looked down. 'Would you like to join us in a real grown-up drink before you go to bed?' he invited. 'Would that be all right, Patsy?'

Tanya nodded her head and Patsy agreed. 'A celebratory drink.'

'Right.' Gavin went across to the drinks cabinet and busied himself with ice and glasses. 'The usual for you?' he said to Patsy, mixing a long gin and lime. 'And what for you, Miss?' He looked at Tanya. 'How about ginger ale on the rocks?'

Tanya looked up at Patsy, and at her slight nod she whispered, 'Yes, please.'

They sat drinking and Gavin raised his glass towards Patsy in a silent toast. 'Do the bubbles get up your nose?' she asked the child, and got a nod in return. The drink finished, Gavin went to shower and change, and Patsy took the child off to bed. 'Goodnight, darling,' she said as she kissed her goodnight, and she added an extra kiss as Tanya whispered, 'Goodnight.' When Elaine arrived a bit later, Gavin told her the news and she smiled at him indulgently.

'You worried about it too much,' she told him. 'The doctors said she would speak again, didn't they? It was just a question of time.'

56

'I guess you're right,' Gavin admitted, 'but I'm very glad the time has come.'

Over the following weeks Tanya spoke more and more. She did not chatter as most children did, but she spoke normally to Patsy during the day, a little shyly to Gavin at night and when they breakfasted together, but to Elaine not at all. Patsy worried about this. She had guessed that Elaine must be the 'someone' to whom Gavin had referred in England, and if they were to marry, how would Tanya fare? Elaine treated the child with a cool friendliness, but never made any effort to come closer to her. On the day after Tanya spoke her first words to them, Patsy decided to keep a diary. Jan had urged her to do so, so that she wouldn't be able to forget the things she had seen and done in Sri Lanka.

'We shall be dying to hear all about it,' she'd said. 'Well I shall write to you of course,' Patsy had replied, but now, because of both her nurse's and teacher's training, she decided to keep a diary which would be chiefly a record of Tanya's progress. It would be a good idea, she thought, to keep a record of her progress in other ways too. She was four years old now, and perhaps ready to learn a few simple things in preparation for when she had to go to school.

As Gavin had said, she gradually met his friends. Several of them were married couples and some of them had children, so that gradully Tanya built up a small circle of friends too. Among his unmarried friends a tall red-head named Barney Morley made the greatest impression on her. She guessed that Barney was probably short for Barnabas, but as everyone seemed to call him just 'Red', she did too. He was obviously very interested in Patsy; as he said later, he fell in love with her the first time he saw her sitting on the floor dressing dolls with Tanya; and from the time of that first meeting he haunted the house whenever he was free. He asked Patsy to go out to dinner with him, and Gavin insisted that she went. 'Tanya is not nearly so clinging to you now,' he said, 'and if she wakes up, which she usually doesn't do, I expect she'll be content with me, if I tell her you'll soon be back.'

So Patsy went into Colombo to dine with Red, and it was the first of many pleasant evenings spent in his company. He worked for the British Council, he told her, and was mostly concerned with education. They found that as well as education they had a great many other common interests, and the time she spent with him seemed to fly past. She also met Elaine's brother, Peter, with whom Elaine lived in a flat in Colombo itself. He was tall and blond but didn't resemble his sister in any other way. He, too, dated Patsy, and she dined with him several times. Mostly he took her to interesting places out in the country. He was good-looking, charming and attentive, but

Patsy always preferred her outings with Red. Peter dealt in emeralds and other precious stones, he told her when she asked, and his business often took him away to other parts of Sri Lanka. 'This country is more prolific in jewels than almost any other in the world for its size,' he told her. 'There are no diamonds found here, but almost every other kind of stone, and the emeralds and sapphires are the best in the world.'

Patsy found that she was thoroughly enjoying her new life, and as she wrote her diary before she went to bed each night she realised how very different it was from the one she had left. As the summer heat intensified she enjoyed that, too, and as Tanya didn't seem in any way affected by it, Patsy refused Gavin's offer to send them both to stay in one of the cooler hill stations, Kandy or Nuwar-Eliya until the summer was over.

'You ought to see some of those places, though,' he remarked. 'We'll arrange to go for a few days when I'm not quite so busy.'

The only slight cloud that marred Patsy's days was the presence of Elaine. She always spent the weekends at Gavin's house, and was there several nights a week. Tanya was quieter and clung to Patsy a bit more at those times. Gavin noticed it and tried unobtrusively to bring them closer. Elaine made no special efforts, but Patsy, wondering if her own dislike of the other girl was being reflected by the child, tried to be more friendly and talkative with her. Elaine, however, seemed to have eyes only for Gavin, and she replied briefly to Patsy's overtures. It was obvious that there was no other woman in Gavin's life, but there had been no mention of an engagement, and Elaine did not wear a ring. 'Perhaps he's waiting,' Patsy thought, 'until he sees how she does get on with Tanya. After all, if they marry the responsibility for Tanya will be hers as well.' And yet, Elaine's behaviour towards Gavin was very proprietorial. Perhaps they didn't believe in engagements, and one day they would just announce that they were going to marry. Patsy found that at this thought her hands clenched so tightly that the nails cut her palms, and she relaxed slowly. She looked across to the bar where Gavin was mixing them a second drink; Elaine had leaned back in her chair and was watching him too. 'Make mine a weak one, darling,' she said. 'If we're going on to the Greys' party, I'd better not drink too much before we start.' Patsy felt a sudden rush of an emotion that she did not recognise, and looking down at Tanya who was sitting on the floor and doing a jigsaw puzzle, she said, 'Come on, poppet, bedtime.'

Gavin looked at her. 'Isn't it a bit early?' he asked.

'We're having an extra-long story tonight,' Patsy said hastily as the little girl obediently scrambled to her feet. 'Say goodnight to

Elaine and Uncle Gavin.'

He crossed the room with his long stride to pick Tanya up and hug her. 'Goodnight, sweetheart,' he said. 'I think I'm going to come with you one night and hear one of these fascinating stories Patsy tells you.'

'We've got a new book and she reads some,' Tanya told him. He set her on her feet as she added, 'I'm going to learn to read, too, Patsy says.'

'That'll be lovely. Then you'll be able to read stories to me. Goodnight, love. Off you go.'

'Goodnight, Uncle Gavin.'

'And goodnight, Elaine,' Patsy prompted.

'Goodnight,' Tanya murmured obediently, not looking at the other girl.

'What story are we going to have?' she asked, when she had cleaned her teeth and climbed into bed.

'You choose,' Patsy suggested, with her mind far from Tanya and bedtime stories.

'But you said an extra-long one.'

'Well, we could have two stories instead.'

'Will you read to me out of the book you sometimes write in?'

Patsy realised that Tanya meant the diary in which she had sometimes jotted down incidents during the daytime as well as her regular entries at night.

'All right,' she agreed, 'but it's not as good as a story.'

She fetched her diary and riffled through the pages to find something suitable to read to a child, and settled on a description of an afternoon they had spent with Red in driving out to an old ruined temple and picnicking nearby.

'It's all about us.' Tanya was surprised. 'Read some more.' She was entranced with these descriptions of things they had done, and asked to be shown where her name was written.

'You could write your name too,' Patsy told her. 'Tomorrow I'll show you how to do it; but now it's time for you to go to sleep.'

Tanya obediently snuggled down under the thin sheet which was all the covering she needed and Patsy went through to her own room. She sank into the chair by the window and clasped her hands over her fast-beating heart. As she had read to Tanya and answered her questions, she had suddenly realised that the emotions which had swept over her as she watched Gavin and Elaine had been sheer jealousy. 'I'm in love with him,' she told herself slowly. 'I want to be the one to call him darling, and to keep catching his hands, and leaning against his shoulder.' She stared unseeing out of the window and let the full implication of this wash over her. 'I think I've always been a bit in love with him ever since we first met and spent those few days together with Tanya, and now being here and seeing him every day it has grown and grown.' All her resentment and dislike of Elaine, she thought, probably stemmed from this, but perhaps also a little because of the other girl's complete indifference to the child. 'If she really loved Gavin surely she would make some effort to get on with Tanya,' she thought. She found that her hands were trembling, and clasped them even tighter in her lap. Pictures of Gavin flashed before her eyes. Gavin as she had first seen him, crouching beside Tanya and pointing to things in the toy-shop window; Gavin as he sat opposite her at the breakfast table; Gavin in the pool with Tanya; and Gavin walking across the room towards her to bring her a drink. Elaine was in none of these pictures, but Patsy was powerless to stop her intrusion, and against her will she saw Elaine leaning back in her chair, calling Gavin 'darling' and reminding him that they would be together for the rest of the evening. Her imagination took over and she thought of Gavin kissing Elaine goodnight when he took her home. Did he go in? How long did he stay? What did they talk about? Were they perhaps even now planning for the time when they would marry? 'How blind I've been not to realise before that I want Gavin for myself. Just Gavin and me and Tanya, and perhaps later—' She jumped to her feet and stood leaning out of the window. She must not think like this. Gavin was polite and friendly to her, but he never given even the slightest sign that

63

he thought anything special of her. Oh, he had called her a guardian angel, true, but that was out of gratitude for all she had done for Tanya. 'I don't want his gratitude.' she thought rebelliously. 'I want his love. I want him to hurry home because he can't wait to see me, not just to be with Tanya for a little while before she goes to bed. I want—' Her thoughts were interrupted by Gavin's shout from below her window, and she blushed suddenly as if he were able to read her thoughts. 'We're just off, Patsy. 'Bye, see you at breakfast tomorrow if you've gone to bed before I get back. The Greys' parties usually go on for ever.' Elaine waved briefly without saying anything, and Patsy returned the wave without saying anything. As she watched the car go down the short drive, she remembered with dismay that Red was coming to have dinner with her. Usually she was glad to see him, but tonight she would have preferred to be alone with her thoughts.

She crossed to the bed and picked up her diary. 'I've always been rather amused at the thought of people talking to their diaries,' she thought, 'but now I can understand it when there's no-one else to talk to.' She picked up a pen from her bedside table and wrote, 'I love Gavin ORourke.' For a moment she just sat and looked at what she had written and then she snapped the book shut and prepared to go down to greet Red.

CHAPTER SIX

Gavin had left the second drink that he had been mixing on the little table beside her usual chair, and she added more ice and sat sipping it and trying to regain her composure. After about five minutes she heard Red's car draw up and put down her glass to go and meet him. He ran up the steps to the verandah, and crossed quickly to her side. 'Red does everything at a run,' she thought as he reached her side and gave her a brief hug.

'I thought I'd get here before Gavin and Elaine left,' he greeted her, 'but I got held up by the traffic.'

'Did you specially want to see them?' she asked, and he answered cheerfully:

'Oh no, but as I am his guest, as it were, I thought I ought at least to say thank you. Still, it's better like this, it gives me a good excuse to stay until he comes back.'

'They've gone to somebody called Grey,' Patsy told him, 'and he seemed to think he'd be very late back.'

'Suits me,' Red grinned. 'Shall I get myself a drink?'

'Yes please. You know just how you like it.'

During their meal together and afterwards Patsy exerted herself to be companionable and entertaining, and tried to keep her most important thoughts and feelings at bay. Red told her about a new scheme they had for giving help to largely inexperienced Singhalese teachers.

'We're getting people to give demonstration lessons,' he said, 'and also experienced teachers to come and give informal talks. Would you come, Patsy?'

'What, to talk you mean?' she asked incredulously.

'Yes. Some of the teachers of young children would benefit enormously from what you could tell them.'

'Oh heavens, Red,' she said, surprised. 'I don't think I could do that. 'I don't know anything special, and I'd feel a bit odd telling people what to do.'

'You don't need to know anything special,' he assured her, 'just your attitude to young children is what we want to get over. They tend to have them sitting in rows and learning things by rote. They just don't understand how much children can learn from a more informal approach; please say you will, Patsy. I could go over with you first what you want to say, what you feel they ought to know, and I'm sure they would benefit from it.'

'Well, I'd like to help you, but I'm not sure—'

'Tell you what,' he said suddenly. 'You could come with me to visit a few schools, and then you'd see what's needed, and I'm sure you'd be able to put it over. They're all so eager to learn. We want to give them all the help we can.'

'All right,' Patsy agreed. 'I suppose I could try.'

'Thank you. Now that's enough about teachers. Let's talk about us. How are you really liking Sri Lanka, Patsy?'

'I love it,' she told him truthfully. 'I can't imagine living anywhere else now.'

'That's super,' his voice was warm, 'but what about your family, how do they feel about it?'

'I haven't really got any family,' she told him. 'Both my mother and father are dead, and I have no brothers or sisters. In fact the only relative I have is an old aunt who lives in Yorkshire and whom I haven't seen for so long that I can't even remember her.'

'So you would be quite willing to go on living here?'

'Well, I don't plan to leave just yet,' she told him with a smile, while at the back of her mind she imagined what it would be like to live here always with Gavin.

'I'm very glad about that, Patsy,' he said, his voice suddenly serious. 'You must know how I feel about you, and although I haven't known you for years, I know very definitely that you are the person I want to spend the rest of my life with.' Patsy stared at him. 'Oh, I know I'm rushing it,' Red went on. 'I intended to wait for ages before I mentioned it to you, but I love

you so much I'm impatient, Patsy, and—and—
you're not entirely indifferent to me, are you?'

'I like you very much,' Patsy said slowly, 'but
I—'

'Well, that's a good start,' he said. 'And I
really won't try to rush you, love. I just
somehow had to let you know what I feel.
Right now my biggest ambition in life is to get
you to agree to marry me.'

Patsy was silent. She liked Red very much
indeed, but it was a pale emotion indeed
compared with her feeling for Gavin.
Remembering her feelings for Gavin, however,
she found it hard to wipe the look of eager
hope from Red's face. 'You might get around
to loving me, Patsy,' he urged. 'Anyhow, now
you know how I feel, and any time you want to
I'll be thrilled and honoured to marry you.'

'Thank you, Red,' was all she could think of
to say. 'But I don't love you, and although I
like you very much, that isn't enough for a
marriage.'

'Well at least you'll go on seeing me, won't
you?'

'Perhaps I shouldn't,' she murmured, but he
interrupted at once.

'It won't bind you to anything, love. Please
let me go on seeing you, and who knows, you
might suddenly find that you do love me after
all.'

Remembering how suddenly she had found
that she loved Gavin, Patsy didn't contradict

him; she was indeed very fond of Red, and there was no future for her with Gavin. Perhaps in time her feelings for Red would grow stronger. For the rest of the evening they chatted of inconsequential things, and when at half past ten Patsy pleaded tiredness, he left without demur. She went immediately to her room, but not to bed. In spite of what she had said to Red, she had never felt less tired in her life. Her mind was a whirl of conflicting thoughts and emotions. How could she go on living under the same roof as Gavin now that she had admitted to herself how much she loved him? There was no going back now and she could deceive herself no longer. It would be exquisite torture to sit opposite to him at the breakfast table, and to watch out for his arrival home at night. Yet how could she leave? Both he and Tanya depended on her. It was a small comfort to know how much they did depend on her. At least in continuing to look after the child she was doing something for him; but what about when he married Elaine? Then, she thought, she would really have to go. As she slowly prepared for bed she resolved that she would try harder to make Tanya and Elaine get on better together. She looked in on the sleeping child, and then got into her own bed where she tossed and turned, unable to find sleep or any peace of mind. She was still awake when Gavin came home at two o'clock. Had he been at the party until then,

69

she wondered, or had he been alone somewhere with Elaine? Resolutely she tried to put such thoughts out of her mind, but it was a long time before she fell into a fitful sleep, and she awoke in the morning feeling more tired than when she had gone to bed.

Gavin and Tanya talked cheerfully at breakfast and neither seemed to notice how quiet and withdrawn Patsy was.

'I shall be home for lunch today,' Gavin told them, 'so perhaps we could do something together this afternoon when Tanya's had her rest.' The child's eyes lighted up, and Patsy clasped her hands beneath the table. The moments she could spend alone with him were precious, but they also turned the knife in the wound of knowing that he loved another woman.

'Will Elaine come?' Tanya asked in her soft voice.

'Not today,' he answered, and turning to Patsy he added, 'I'm giving Elaine more to do with the export and advertising side of things. She really has a remarkable head for business. I might as well let her use it. She obviously enjoys it, and it will give me more time for other things. I must go and visit both plantations for instance; so I'm going to make full use of Elaine and what she enjoys doing while I've got her there. I won't have her for ever to help in the office, marriage is sure to interfere.' Patsy sat quite still. This was the first time he had mentioned marriage and she wondered what they had decided. By what he had said, Elaine would give up working once they were married, and that would mean that she and the other girl would see much more of each other. But how could she stay on once they were married? It would be unbearable! She became aware that Gavin was speaking to her again and she dragged her mind back to the present.

'—decide what we'll do,' she heard, and there and then he put down his table napkin, bent over to kiss Tanya and was gone.

'What shall we do with Uncle Gavin?' Tanya asked. 'He said we can choose.'

'What would you like to do?'

'Could we go in his car? We might see some more donkeys and some elephants like we did before.'

'All right,' Patsy agreed. 'We'll ask him to take us for a drive.' During the morning she toyed with the idea of asking him to take the child alone, and pleading that she had things to do; but as it grew nearer to lunchtime she knew that she could not bear to give up a few hours in his company, and so, at three o'clock, when Tanya had had the briefest possible rest, they set out.

'I'll sit in the back with Tanya,' Patsy said as Gavin opened the car doors for them. 'Then I can point things out to her as we go along.'

'Oh. All right.' He seemed surprised, but

Patsy was glad to be spared the intimacy of sitting so close beside him.

'Was it a good party last night?' she ventured as they started off.

'Not bad, I suppose. I don't really enjoy those noisy gatherings, but Elaine seems to love them.'

'Where are we going?' Tanya wanted to know.

'I thought we'd drive up to the nearest rest-house, which is a sort of little hotel built for travellers in the old days, and we could have tea there before we come back. Jack Bryant, the manager, has an aviary of birds that you might like to see.'

He drove along at a steady pace and Tanya exclaimed over everything they saw. What a pleasure it was to hear her talking, Patsy thought. Except for her shyness, and the way she closed up like a flower at night-time when Elaine was present, she was just like any other four-year-old. She resolutely put Elaine out of her mind, and resolved to enjoy this afternoon as much as she could. It would be something to remember, she told herself, in the bleak times that were sure to come.

'Look! Look!' Tanya commanded. 'There are a lot of men paddling!' Gavin obligingly stopped the car, and they looked at the row of men in their breech-cloths bending over in the water.

'They're not just paddling, they're working,'

he told her. 'They're planting rice. There's a lot of rice grown around here.'

'But why are they in the water?' Tanya was puzzled.

'Rice has to be planted in water,' he told her, and murmured in an aside to Patsy, 'I hope she doesn't want a complete run-down, because that's all I know.' Tanya, however, was satisfied with his answer, and merely remarked wonderingly:

'They don't have much clothes on.'

'I expect it's hot work,' Patsy explained.

A few miles further on they stopped again, this time to watch some elephants bathing in a little stream. There were three big elephants and a baby with which Tanya was enchanted. The huge animals squirted water over themselves and each other, and the man who was with them brushed their thick grey hide with a long-handled stiff brush.

'Why do they have to have a bath?' Tanya wanted to know.

'They've been working, too, I expect,' Gavin told her. 'When a lot of trees have to be cleared away to make room to plant things, the elephants knock them down.'

'Because they're so big and strong?'

'That's right, because they're so big and strong; and they get hot and tired, so when they've finished they come to the river and have a nice bath.'

'The little one doesn't work, does he?'

'No, but he likes to be with his mother, and I expect she likes to have him with her.' Tanya was silent for a minute and her hand crept into Patsy's.

'I wouldn't like to be scrubbed with that big brush, would you?' Patsy said cheerfully, 'but the elephants have got such a thick skin that they don't mind it.'

'We could have an elephant to water the garden,' Tanya said after a while, and Gavin laughed.

'I suppose we could,' he agreed, 'but those big feet would make an awful mess of the flower-beds, wouldn't they?'

Tanya giggled at the thought. 'But it would be nice to have an elephant,' she insisted.

'I have a much better idea than that,' he told her. 'The man we are going to see sometimes has some puppies for sale. If Patsy agrees, how would you like a puppy?'

'Oh yes!' Tanya's eyes grew round with excitement. 'Could we, Patsy?'

'If you help to look after it, I'm sure we could,' Patsy agreed.

'I'll look after it all,' Tanya assured her fervently.

'We may have to wait awhile,' Gavin warned her. 'He might not have any puppies just now, but if he doesn't, we'll tell him that we'd like one the next time he gets some.' Tanya wriggled with excitement, and Patsy thought lovingly how good Gavin was with the child. It couldn't be easy for a man suddenly to assume the full responsibility for a young child, especially as he had had no earlier experience of children, but Gavin seemed to understand just how to treat the little girl, and he seemed to love her as much as if she were his own. At the thought of Gavin having children of his own Patsy felt a momentary pang of pain. Perhaps there wouldn't be any more children. Somehow she couldn't imagine the sophisticated Elaine with a baby.

'When will we get there?' Tanya was asking in a fever of impatience. 'How far is it?' Her mind was now exclusively on the puppy that might soon be hers, and she paid scant attention to anything that Patsy pointed out along the way. When they reached the rest-house and Gavin introduced them to the big man who came out to meet them, she forgot her customary shyness and asked him at once, 'Please, do you have any puppies?'

'Well, yes I do,' he answered, smiling down at her. 'Would you like to come and see them? They're very little, only two weeks old.'

'That means they're not big enough to be taken away yet,' Gavin told her, 'but we'll go and look at them and if Mr Bryant says we can buy one, perhaps you could choose which one you would like to have.'

The mother of the puppies was an indeterminate mixture, more collie than anything else. 'If you have one of my puppies you'll have to look after it well,' Jack Bryant told the eager little girl as they looked down at the wriggling little creatures. 'You can see what a long coat their mother has. They'll be like that too, and they'll need to be well brushed every day.'

Tanya was kneeling down beside the mother and puppies and Gavin instinctively crouched down beside her.

'It's all right,' the other man assured him. 'Old Jess is as good as gold. She'd never hurt a child. Would you like to hold one of them?' he added, to Tanya.

'Oh yes please. That one.' She pointed to what looked like the biggest and strongest of the puppies, who was crawling over his brothers and sisters in search of nourishment. He picked the puppy up and handed it to her and she sat cradling it on her knee, while the adults looked on indulgently, and the old dog slowly wagged her tail. At last they were able to drag the child away from the dogs and go to have some tea, but her mind was obviously still on the puppies and she sat quietly, taking no notice of the grown-ups' talk.

'I was very sorry to hear about your brother,' Jack Bryant said quietly. 'It must be eight or nine years since I saw him. I remember when your father died and you took over the business, he decided he wanted to go to England and live there.' Patsy sat as quietly as Tanya while the two men reminisced, and talked about the tea plantations.

'Everything's doing very well,' Gavin said. 'I've got two big new contracts and I think that I shall have to open up more land.'

'That's good; and what about other things? Are you going to get married now that you're a family man?'

Patsy waited, holding her breath for his answer.

'I've thought about it a lot,' Gavin replied slowly, 'but I don't want to rush things.'

'Well, don't forget to invite me to the wedding.'

'Don't worry, I won't. Now I guess we'd better start back. Tanya, do you want to have one more look at the puppies, and perhaps see Mr Bryant's birds before we leave?'

All three of them were fairly silent on the drive home. Tanya was wondering how long it would be before they could go back and they could carry away that lovely furry bundle of puppy. Patsy was wondering with an aching heart how long it would be before Gavin decided he had waited long enough, and no-one knew what Gavin himself was thinking.

CHAPTER SEVEN

Wanting to have a clear memory of this afternoon they had spent together, Patsy wrote about it in her diary. She made it just a factual account of what they had seen and done, knowing that she didn't need to record her feelings. She read it out to Tanya a few nights later in place of the usual bedtime story and the child was delighted, and in the days that followed she often asked for 'the bit about the puppies'. Gavin said that he was going away for a few days. 'I must take a quick look at both plantations,' he told Patsy, 'and see which one would be most suitable for enlarging. I've definitely got to open up some more ground. I thought that perhaps when the work actually starts you and Tanya could come up for a day, and she could see the elephants working.'

'She'd love that,' Patsy agreed, 'and so would I.'

'Also, when I come back I want you to have more free time for yourself,' he surprised her by saying.

'But I don't need any more free time,' she protested. 'I can go out almost any evening I want, and my work is certainly not hard.'

'All the same, I think you should be able to go off for the day sometimes without Tanya. She's quite happy with me, and she gets on very well with Mrs Jancsz, who would obviously spoil her terribly if she got the chance.'

'But—'

'No buts,' he interrupted firmly. 'Red is always here at weekends, and I know he'd like to take you off for the day instead of sharing you with us. You do like him, don't you, Patsy?'

'Yes, yes I do—'

'Well that's settled then. Make it Saturday or Sunday, whichever you like. There's Peter too,' he added, 'he seems to be quite often queueing up for a date with you.'

'When are you leaving?' Patsy changed the subject.

'I'll go today and I'll come back the day after tomorrow. You'll be all right, won't you?'

'Of course we will,' she assured him, and half an hour later she and Tanya stood on the verandah and waved goodbye.

The house seemed oddly empty with just the knowledge that Gavin would not be back that night, and Patsy was glad when Red telephoned and asked if he could come over for a while. Dear Red, perhaps he had guessed that she would like company. He had really kept his word and had not again mentioned marriage. A future with him, she thought, would be very pleasant.

During the evening Red again spoke about Patsy coming to talk to some of the young teachers. 'They just need a few pointers,' he told her. 'They really do care about the children, but they are still clinging to the old-fashioned way in which they were educated. If you can put over to them that young children really learn by doing and not by being told, you would be doing a very real service.' Together they went over what points she would raise when she talked to the teachers, and Patsy agreed that they would fix a date as soon as Gavin came back.

'I'm sure he wouldn't mind me taking Tanya with me,' she said, 'but I'd like to ask him first.'

She told Red about Gavin's suggestion that she should have more free time, and he was delighted.

'I'd like to take you to see my house,' he said. 'It's about ten miles out of Colombo, and I'm very proud of my garden.'

Tanya was missing Gavin too, and at intervals all the next day she asked when he was coming back. In the evening after the child had gone to bed, Patsy was surprised by a visit from Peter.

'Hallo,' he said as he came up to the verandah. 'Am I welcome or are you expecting other company?'

'No, come in,' Patsy said unnecessarily. 'Have you eaten? I've just finished dinner, but I'm sure Mrs Jancsz could find something for you.'

'I've had dinner, thanks. I've just come from

the club. I felt lonely and I thought perhaps you might too, so I came to see. When is Gavin coming back?'

'Tomorrow I think, but I'm not sure what time.'

'Well,' Peter said, sinking into a chair opposite her, 'how's everything in your world? Tell me what's been going on.'

'Everything's fine with me,' Patsy lied. 'I seem to lead a very lazy life, and I love living here. Everything is so bright and colourful. Quite different from England. How long have you lived here?' she changed the subject.

'About a year,' he told her—'I'm a restless soul and I don't like staying too long in one place.'

'Where were you before?'

'In South Africa.'

'Did you like it there?'

'It was all right I suppose, but I haven't yet found anywhere I'd like to settle down. Perhaps I've got gypsy blood in me,' he laughed.

'Oh I'm sorry, I haven't offered you a drink.' Patsy jumped to her feet and crossed the room. 'What would you like?'

'I'll have a whisky and soda, thanks.' Peter came and stood beside her at the bar, and watched as she mixed his drink.

'Is that all right?' she asked as she handed him the glass. 'Have I put enough whisky in?'

He laughed and leaned forward and kissed

her forehead before he took the proffered drink. 'It's perfect, thanks,' he smiled. 'You're very sweet, Patsy. Sometimes you're like a little girl playing at being grown up.'

Patsy blushed. 'Oh dear, I'm not sure I like that. I think I'm quite grown up.'

'Yes of course you are. I'm only teasing. You're quite grown up and very attractive. Too attractive to be hidden away in this backwater. How can you ever meet anyone here.'

'But I've met lots of people,' she protested. 'I think I know more people here than I did in England.'

'Oh yes, you probably do, but mostly they're stuffy old married people. You're too young for that. You ought to be surrounded by young people, and have loads of boyfriends. How many boyfriends have you got, Patsy?'

'People aren't necessarily boring because they're married,' Patsy avoided his question.

'How many boyfriends have you got?' he repeated, with a gleam in his eyes. 'Would you count me as one? I'd like you to.' Patsy felt embarrassed.

'It's a silly expression, "boy friend", isn't it?' she said lightly. 'It really must mean a friend who happens to be male.'

'Well, I happen to be male,' he teased, 'and I sometimes feel very male when I'm with you. What do you say, Patsy? Will you have me for a boyfriend?'

'This is a silly conversation.' She tried to

end it, feeling confused and uncomfortable under his mocking gaze.

'All right,' he responded, with mock solemnity. 'What would you like to talk about?'

'Tell me about your job,' Patsy said, grasping at this straw to cover her discomfort.

'My job; well it's dealing with precious stones, you already know that.'

'Do you like it?'

'I love it,' he said with a fervency that surprised her. 'They're so beautiful, so pure and lovely. Diamonds, rubies, emeralds, sapphires—' His voice trailed away and he smiled at her. 'Besides which,' he added, 'they are very valuable.'

'You said once before that Sri Lanka is very rich in jewels.'

'It is,' he confirmed. 'It's a very small country, but it produces an amazing range of jewels. There are emeralds, rubies, sapphires, topaz, and pearls from the north. There aren't any diamonds, those I was dealing with in South Africa.'

'Which do you like best?' Patsy relaxed a little, thinking that she was on safer ground.

'Oh, emeralds and diamonds, I think; but you should wear topaz, Patsy. Topaz jewellery would suit your colouring. Come to think of it you're like a topaz yourself; a charming jewel on the surface but with hidden depths. I'm sure you've got hidden depths, haven't you,

Patsy?'

'I guess everyone has,' she replied, as lightly as she could. She had never before seen Peter in this mood. His voice was light and teasing, but she felt as if he were playing with her as a cat does with a mouse.

'Ah, but I'm not interested in everyone,' he countered, 'only in you.' He crossed the room and sat beside her.

'You're so cool and calm on the outside,' he said, 'treating us all as if we were small children like young Tanya; it'll be a lucky someone who disturbs your calm, and gets to see the real Patsy. I'd like it to be me.' He slid his arm along the back of the settee and around her shoulders. 'What do you say?' he whispered. 'Would you wake up for me, little flower?' Before she had time to move or say anything his arms were around her, holding her tightly, and his lips were closing over hers. She felt a moment of panic and as his lips grew more demanding she tried to struggle away from him. Her efforts only served to tighten his hold, and he leaned right across her, pressing her back on to the settee.

'I'm sorry to interrupt but I'd like to come in!' An icy voice made Peter release her hastily and turn towards the door. Gavin stood there, small suitcase in hand and a look of distaste on his face. Peter straightened up and Patsy pulled down her skirt which had become disarranged in her struggle to get free. Her eyes met Gavin's across the room.

'I—I thought you weren't coming back till tomorrow,' she stammered, unable to think of anything else to say.

'Obviously.' His voice was curt. Peter gave a low laugh.

'Well now that you've come, I'd better go,' he said, and with a mocking glance at Patsy, and a cheerful, 'Goodnight, sweetheart,' he got to his feet. There was a silence until they heard his footsteps go down the verandah steps and then Patsy spoke to Gavin.

'It was—I mean he—' she began, but he interrupted her with an impatient gesture.

'Oh for heaven's sake don't start explaining,' he said. 'It was perfectly obvious what it was. I'm tired. I'm going to bed. Goodnight.' And before Patsy could say anything else he had left the room.

She stood staring after him with tears gathering in her brown eyes. What did he think, and why, oh why, had she blurted out what she did? She rubbed the back of her hand across her mouth which felt bruised from Peter's kiss. Her hands trembled a little and she felt that she wanted to rush after Gavin and say, 'It's not like you think. I didn't want him to kiss me. I was trying to make him stop.' But how could she do that? She imagined Gavin's cold voice saying, 'Why explain? It's not my business what you do with Peter.' And she saw again the look of distaste which had

85

been on his face. Wearily she put off the lights and went to her own room, where the tears which had threatened downstairs overflowed, and she lay sobbing on her bed. It was some time before she could control her crying and get ready for bed, and even longer before she was able to sleep.

When she awoke in the morning her head thumped and her throat felt dry and sore. Tanya was sitting patiently on the end of her bed.

'You slept a long time, Patsy,' she said accusingly. 'I got dressed all by myself and went downstairs, but Uncle Gavin said not to wake you, so I didn't.'

'Sorry, poppet. I'll get up now. Have you had your breakfast?'

'No. I waited for you.'

'Well I'll be very quick and then we'll have it together.'

As she dressed Patsy felt glad that Gavin had already left. It would have been difficult to face him calmly across the breakfast table. How would he behave when they did meet in the evening, and should she bring up the subject again? Listening with one ear to what the child was saying, Patsy decided that the best thing would be to carry on as if the incident had never happened, and hope that it would soon be forgotten. She resolved however to avoid Peter as much as she could.

This resolve was squashed almost at once as

Gavin phoned her during the morning, and in a perfectly ordinary voice told her that he would be bringing both Elaine and Peter back to dinner. 'Will you tell Mrs Jancsz?' he asked, 'and apologise for me for the short notice.'

'Yes, I will,' she answered, 'and Gavin—'

'Yes?'

'I'm sorry I was late up this morning.'

'It doesn't matter in the least,' his cool voice assured her. 'See you tonight.'

Patsy went through to the kitchen to tell the housekeeper, and to ask if she could help.

'Bless you, no.' The answer was cheerful. 'There's no problem in cooking for a few extra. Don't worry, Miss Patsy, I'll see to it all. How about you now, Miss Tanya? Would you like a piece of my home-made fudge?'

Patsy went through the day in an inner turmoil. How would she meet both Peter and Gavin, and why had he chosen tonight of all nights to invite them? They were a little late in arriving and Tanya had already had her bath and was in her night-clothes.

'Patsy said I could wait up and have my evening drink with you before I go to bed,' she told Gavin as she greeted him.

'Good,' he responded, picking her up to hug her. 'What will you have? The usual?'

Tanya giggled. 'Yes please.'

'And the usual for everyone else, I presume?' Gavin glanced round at them all. Patsy felt Peter's mocking glance on her but

87

she studiously avoided his eyes, and gathered up the picture-books at which she and Tanya had been looking. There was a little silence as they all settled back with their drinks, and Patsy found it oppressive. She turned to Tanya and said:

'Wouldn't you like to show Uncle Gavin and Elaine the pictures you coloured?' The child obediently picked out one of the books and took it across to Gavin.

'And Elaine,' Patsy insisted gently. Tanya held the book out to Elaine but remained leaning against Gavin's knee.

'Very nice.' Elaine dismissed it with a glance, and it was left to Gavin to make more fulsome comments. Patsy gave a little sigh. She was trying so hard to make Elaine and Tanya more compatible, but Tanya just woodenly did as she was told and Elaine seemed to make no effort at all.

'If you've finished your drink I think I'd better take you up to bed,' she said. 'Say goodnight to everyone.'

'If you'll excuse me I must disappear for a minute or two as well,' Gavin said, getting to his feet. 'There's a phone call I should have made before I left the office, and I must do it tonight.' He followed Patsy and Tanya from the room and went towards his study.

Tanya was tired and for once was content with one story before she settled herself for sleep. Patsy kissed her goodnight and went softly down the stairs. As she neared the verandah where they had been sitting, she heard Peter's voice slightly raised as if in anger, and involuntarily she paused.

'Can't you take a bit more notice of the kid?' he was saying. 'You're going to lose his interest if you don't.'

Elaine's mocking voice answered lightly: 'I won't lose his interest. Don't worry. You do your job and I'll do mine; and incidentally I notice that the girl is a bit embarrassed tonight. I hope you haven't been playing about with her. That's not necessary.'

'Oh Elaine. You know me. I'm getting restless and bored. It's time I moved on.'

'But Peter—'

At that moment Gavin came out of his study and Patsy moved on down the stairs. She had not meant to eavesdrop, but what she had overheard was disconcerting and puzzling. Gavin had obviously not heard anything, but as she joined him and the others she wondered what was the meaning of what she had heard.

CHAPTER EIGHT

She turned it over in her mind for the next few days, but she was more preoccupied with her own feelings and with Gavin's attitude. She did not see anything of Peter, for which she was heartily glad. Gavin never mentioned him either, but he seemed very distant and overly polite. He did not object to her taking Tanya to one of Red's little schools, and both she and the child enjoyed the visit. They went with Red one afternoon before the children left school, and as she saw the young children sitting rigidly with their arms folded, Patsy realised what Red had meant.

'All stand,' the young teacher commanded as they entered. As one, the children rose to their feet.

'Say good afternoon,' they were commanded, and in a chorus they obeyed. Red introduced her to the young girl, who looked more like a model than a teacher with her slim figure and beautiful sari. Patsy thought fleetingly that a sari was one of the most flattering garments she had ever seen.

'Will you sit at the back here with me and let Miss Marley talk to your class?' Red called and the girl nodded shyly.

'Of course,' she said softly.

Patsy pulled a chair to the front of the class

and sat on it. 'Come and sit here on the floor beside me,' she beckoned. 'I'm going to tell you a story.'

The children shuffled their feet uncomfortably and looked to their teacher for guidance in the face of this strange request. She nodded her head and reinforced it. 'Come,' she said, and as Tanya sat at Patsy's feet they slowly came and joined her. Patsy leaned forward and looked into the little faces turned up to hers. 'I'm going to tell you a story about a monkey,' she began. 'Who's seen a monkey?' Shyly a few hands crept up.

'I have,' Tanya announced. 'I saw one when I went to the zoo with Patsy and Uncle Gavin.'

'Sh,' a few children reproached her.

'No, that's good.' Patsy smiled her approval. 'Tell me about it, Tanya.' As the child launched into a description of the day at the zoo, Patsy looked at her fondly and thought what a different child she was from the silent little creature she had first met. These children were a bit like that, she thought, but they had been taught to listen and not talk. She hoped that she could encourage them a bit, and also encourage their teacher to give them a bit more freedom. It was uphill work, but gradually she elicited a few responses from them, and with Tanya's help she got them to participate. The naughty monkey took fruit from the market, she told them, he took washing from the line, he took the hat from a man who was standing and waiting for a bus, and every time he took something the people shouted, 'Come back, naughty monkey. Come back.'

'What did the people say,' she asked when she had told how the monkey stole the hat.

'Naughty monkey. Come back,' Tanya said.

'That's right,' Patsy approved. 'Now everybody tell me.' With giggles and shy smiles a few children obliged, and after the next theft when Patsy asked, 'What did the people say?' a few more joined in. She went on with the story, making it up as she went along and trying to bring in things and episodes with which the children would be familiar. When she had finished she sent them back to their seats and gave out paper and bright crayons she had brought with her. I want you to draw me a picture,' she told them. 'Something from the story. Perhaps the naughty monkey. Who can draw a monkey?'

'I can,' Tanya announced, but there was only silence from the others. Their teacher felt embarrassed and intervened.

'You are to draw a monkey.'

'Oh no,' Patsy contradicted her softly. 'I don't want everyone to draw a monkey. Perhaps someone would draw the hat that he took, or the bananas, or anything else that was in the story.' While Tanya happily drew her picture and the other children gradually grew bold enough to pick up a crayon and attempt something, Patsy talked softly to their teacher.

'They learn so much better by doing things than by just listening,' she said quietly. 'And you will be surprised at how much some of them can learn and how quickly.' She walked round among the children making encouraging remarks about their efforts, and when most of them seemed to have finished, she called a few out to the front of the class to hold up their pictures for the others to see. 'Perhaps some could be pinned up on the wall later on,' she suggested to the teacher. 'But now we could write their names on their pictures and what the picture is, and they could try to copy what we write.'

'We'll do that tomorrow,' the girl promised. 'Now it is time for them to leave.' When the last child had gone Patsy stayed on and talked to the girl, answering her many questions and giving as much advice as she could.

'Thank you. I hope you will return.' After a glance at Red who had been a silent spectator of all this, she nodded.

'I'd like to,' she agreed.

'You were great,' Red enthused, as he drove them home. 'It'll take a long time before there are any real changes, but you've made a beginning and I think that girl is young enough to be open to new ideas.'

Tanya told Gavin all about her afternoon at school, and he smiled indulgently at her vivid little face.

'I guess it won't be too long before it's time for you to go to school,' he said. 'Will you like that?'

Tanya looked doubtful. 'Will Patsy come too?' she asked.

'No, but she'd take you to school and come to meet you when it was time to come home.'

'I think I won't go yet,' she told him, and he laughed.

'Well there's plenty of time,' he agreed, and then he looked from one to the other of them and said, 'Well now, after all you've told me, I've got something to tell you.'

'What is it?' Tanya demanded.

'Well, the elephants have started to knock down the trees for us to plant some more tea bushes, and I thought that perhaps you would like to go and watch them.'

Tanya beamed. 'Oh yes, Uncle Gavin. When can we go? Can we go tomorrow?'

'What do you think, Patsy?' Gavin asked. 'Do you think it would be too tiring for her? I thought we might make it a two-day trip. There's a rest-house about forty miles away from where they are working, and I thought we might spend a night there.'

'Oh yes, Patsy,' Tanya said excitedly. 'We won't be too tired, will we. Can we go tomorrow?'

They both smiled at her enthusiasm, and Patsy agreed that indeed they wouldn't be too tired, and that they would both enjoy it very

94

much.

'We'll ask Mrs Jancsz for an early breakfast and we'll leave at about eight,' Gavin said. 'So maybe you'd better go to bed a bit early, young Tanya.'

'Will you write about the elephants?' the child wanted to know as Patsy took her upstairs.

'If you like, and you can draw some pictures to go with it.'

Downstairs again Patsy was disappointed to find that Gavin was preparing to go out again. 'I have to give Elaine some last-minute instructions,' he said. 'Will you pack whatever you'll both need for two days, and bring swimsuits. They're going to dam the stream that's up there to make a temporary swimming-pool for us.' Patsy's disappointment was lightened by the obvious fact that Elaine would not be going with them, and when Gavin left she went upstairs to pack the few things they would need, before writing about the school visit in her diary and going early to bed herself.

The next two days were perfect, and Patsy thought she would remember them as long as she lived. She had set her little alarm clock to make absolutely sure that she did not oversleep, but there was no danger of that, Tanya was awake and shaking her gently some time before the clock was due to ring. 'We mustn't be late, Patsy,' she urged.

'We won't be,' Patsy assured her as she supervised the dressing and washing and they went down to breakfast. Gavin appeared a few minutes later and smiled at them both.

'You even raced me,' he said, 'and I thought I was very early.' Mrs Jancsz had packed them a substantial picnic lunch and she beamingly watched their departure.

'It's quite a long way,' Gavin warned Tanya, who was already asking when they would arrive.

'There'll be lots of things to see on the way,' Patsy told her, and together they looked out for elephants, bullock-carts and any other things which they had only seen since they had been in this strange and exotic country. At about eleven o'clock they bumped off the road on to a rough track.

'We have to change cars here,' Gavin told them, indicating a Range Rover which stood just off the road with a young man beside it. 'It's going to be too rough now for an ordinary car. Good morning, Sunderaja,' he greeted the young man. 'Have you been waiting long?'

'No boss. Jus' a few minutes,' the young man smiled as he took their small suitcases and the picnic hamper and stowed them away at the back of the Range Rover. Gavin helped Patsy and Tanya into their seats, and Tanya remarked doubtfully, 'It's a bit high up.'

'All the better to see things,' Gavin told her. 'You'll see lots of monkeys from now on. The forest is full of them.'

And indeed they did see monkeys, whole troops of them, clustered at the sides of the rough track they were following, and chattering their disapproval of this intrusion of their territory. Tanya was enchanted and forgot to be nervous as the car bumped and lurched over the rough track.

'There's one with a baby!' she cried. 'Look, Patsy. It's holding on round her neck.'

Sunderaja obligingly stopped for a moment so that they could have a close-up view of the monkey troop. The monkeys were very bold. Some even jumped on to the bonnet to get a closer look at this strange animal which had so suddenly appeared.

'They're not used to people,' Gavin said, 'so they're not scared.'

Long before Tanya had seen her fill of monkeys they started again. 'There'll be lots more,' her uncle told her, 'and if you look carefully you'll see other animals as well.'

The forest was a riot of colour. Giant creepers with brightly-coloured flowers as large as saucers were all along their route, and Patsy noticed some withered and dying where they had been cut back to allow them to pass. There were huge butterflies as brightly coloured as the flowers, and Patsy and Tanya exclaimed again and again in delight. Sunderaja was delighted with their enthusiasm about his country, and he smiled continually and hummed to himself as he skilfully drove the car higher and higher. As they rounded a bend he suddenly stopped and said, 'Look ahead, he is just going to cross the track.' Obediently they peered ahead and were suddenly rewarded when an animal came out from the cover of the bush at the side and began in a leisurely fashion to cross in front of them.

'It's a dragon!' Tanya breathed, with her eyes as round as saucers as she instinctively clutched Patsy's hand.

'What is it?' Patsy asked almost at the same moment.

'It's an iguana,' Gavin told her. 'They grow to be quite big. This one is about medium size.'

'Wow! I'd hate to meet a big one in the dark!'

The animal was about the size of an Alsatian dog, but with shorter legs, and it looked more like a lizard than anything else. There was a row of spikes sticking up along its back which had made Tanya liken it to a dragon. Fascinated, they watched as the creature snuffled across the track and disappeared into the bushes on the other side.

'Only another few minutes and we'll be there,' Gavin told them. 'We have four elephants working, and thank goodness one of them has a baby. I don't think Tanya would have forgiven me if I hadn't produced a baby.'

The Range Rover stopped and they gazed at the scene ahead of them. They had reached a plateau but from somewhere above a little river was splashing down the hillside. On the other side of this a wooden hut had been erected, and from beyond came the crashing sounds of the elephants as they worked, and the shouts of the men in charge of them. Sunderaja went ahead with their cases, Gavin carried Tanya, and Patsy followed apprehensively across the little swaying bridge. Tanya was impatient to see the elephants at work and so they went directly to the scene of action. The huge animals looked even bigger than any they had seen before, and they watched with fascination as, obeying the shouts of the men in charge of them, they tore up trees by their roots and stacked them all in one place.

'It's frightening the destruction they can create,' Patsy almost whispered, and Gavin smiled down at her.

'Yes,' he said. 'I've often thought that. It's good that all that strength is harnessed to something useful. I should imagine that a herd of elephants on the rampage must be truly frightening.'

Tanya would have stayed much longer watching and making excited comments, but Gavin declared that he was starving and that they must go and eat their picnic lunch before he fainted.

He showed them with pride how the little river had been dammed with large tree trunks so as to make a pool large enough for swimming. 'It hasn't stopped the water altogether,' he explained, 'but it's holding it up long enough for the pool to keep full. It's quite shallow at the edge too, so it'll be all right for Tanya.' They found that Sunderaja had unpacked their picnic basket and had stood the bottles of wine and lemonade upright in the water at the side of the pool. 'Good man. We'll have nice cool drinks,' Gavin approved.

'Will he eat with us?'

'No. He'd be embarrassed. He'll cook himself some rice in his hut.'

They sat in the dappled shade of the trees, festooned with creepers and the wonderful flowers, and dangled their feet in the cool water as they ate. Mrs Jancsz had packed them a feast and Patsy thought that never had chicken tasted so good, nor wine felt so heady. When they had finished off with fruit and sat silent and replete, Gavin went into the hut and came out with two blankets.

'I think a little rest is called for,' he said. 'I brought the rugs with me so that we can lie out here in the shade of the trees.'

Tanya was asleep almost at once, and Patsy too felt her eyelids drooping. She awoke after a little while and as her eyes slowly opened she became aware of Gavin beside her, half lying and half sitting, and gazing at her intently.

'Good sleep?' he asked.

'Mm.' Patsy yawned a little. 'This is the life. I can't think how I ever coped with icy-cold mornings and rainy days.'

'Could you face living the rest of your life here with only occasional trips back to England?'

'Oh yes. I love it here.'

'I don't think Red would ever want to live anywhere else,' Gavin remarked, and Patsy was silent.

'But I don't know about Peter,' he went on. 'He's been here a year, but he seems to have travelled quite a lot, and Elaine with him. They're very close for a brother and sister.'

'I've never had a brother or sister so I wouldn't know,' Patsy said shortly. She didn't want to talk about anyone else, she just wanted to enjoy this time alone with Gavin and Tanya. As if he sensed her mood, Gavin didn't mention them again, but went on to tell Patsy something of his early life in Sri Lanka.

'I don't know why my family came out here in the first place,' he said, 'but my grandfather started with one small plantation, and my father built the business up to what it is today.'

'I expect you've added to it a bit?' Patsy suggested, and he nodded.

'Since I've had it we've taken over all the export side ourselves, instead of just passing it on to an export firm,' he agreed. 'It makes for quicker and smoother working. I always wanted to be somewhere about the plantations,' he reminisced, 'but my brother couldn't wait to get away, and he went to England as soon as he was able.'

'And now his daughter's back here,' Patsy said.

'Tell me about you.' Gavin changed the subject. 'You were an only child?'

While Tanya slept they lazily exchanged memories of their childhood, and Patsy thought that she had never felt so close to Gavin, and wished that this afternoon might go on for ever.

CHAPTER NINE

During the afternoon they swam and exchanged desultory remarks. Tanya enjoyed the water, but was anxious to get back to the elephants, so after a while they dressed and walked back to where the huge creatures were still at work. Gavin spread a rug for them on a fallen tree trunk, and they sat and watched until even Tanya had had enough. Except for answering her occasional question they might have been alone, and in the magic afternoon that enfolded them, they talked half to each other and half to themselves.

'I'd never thought much about children until she came to me,' Gavin said, nodding his head towards the entranced child. 'Oh I suppose I just very vaguely thought that perhaps some day I would marry and have a family, but I'd never really thought of children as individuals.'

'You're very good with her.'

He smiled his thanks. 'Coming from an expert like you that's praise indeed,' he said, 'but I realise that when I do have children of my own I must be very, very careful to see to it that she never feels left out.'

Patsy was silent at the thought of Gavin with children of his own, and the talk drifted to other channels.

The shadows began to lengthen, and Gavin

warned Tanya that the work would soon be finished for the day.

'The men will take the elephants to the water now,' he told her. 'We'll go and watch, and then I think we'll have to leave. By the time we get to the rest-house and you've had your dinner it'll be long past your bedtime.' As they watched the elephants wallowing in the water and the mother squirting her baby, he added, 'We could have gone before, but I particularly wanted you to see the sunset, which is really beautiful up here.'

They climbed into the Range Rover and Gavin took the back seat with Tanya. 'You sit in the front,' he said to Patsy. 'We'll be driving due east till we get out on to the main road again, and from the front seat you'll get the best view.'

The colours which were appearing in the sky fully lived up to Gavin's description, and Patsy held her breath at the riot of colour and pattern which filled her view.

'It's wonderful,' she said.

'It doesn't last long though; dark comes quickly here, but I'm glad you've seen it. The sky is pretty at sunset in Colombo, but never quite like here.' There was satisfaction in his voice. By the time they reached the rest-house Tanya was fast asleep, her head on his shoulder. He carried her in as Sunderaja brought the bags and Patsy followed.

'I think I'd better just put her straight to

bed,' Patsy decided. 'She'll probably sleep through till morning.' She was shown to a spotlessly clean small room in which there were two beds, and Tanya hardly awoke as she was undressed. There was a small wash-basin and Patsy washed and prepared to rejoin Gavin. As she combed her hair she looked at herself in the mirror which hung above. Soft brown eyes looked back at her from a face framed by a riot of dark curls, through which she impatiently pulled the comb. 'My nose is too short,' she thought, 'and my skin too brown, and my mouth, well, I suppose it's all right as mouths go, but—' She saw in her mind's eye the smooth blonde hair and the blue eyes of Elaine, and gave a sigh as she put down the comb and put on some lipstick before going to join Gavin. He was waiting for her in the dimly lit little room that passed for lounge and dining-room. 'We're the only guests,' he told her, 'so I expect mine host and his wife will come and chat. It's a fairly lonely life for them nowadays. These rest-houses used to be busy in the old days, but now they don't have many overnight guests, and they've come to be just places to which one drives out to lunch sometimes.'

'Do you know them?'

'Oh yes. I've known them since I was a kid. They're nice people, but I could do without them tonight. I'd much rather just talk to you.'

Patsy hugged the words to herself, thinking

how she would remember them and cherish them.

'I'm not very interesting,' she murmured.

'Oh yes you are. You've got a novel way of looking at lots of things, which sometimes jolts me out of the rut I'm in. I think you're quite a little dark horse, Patsy!'

Fulfilling Gavin's prophecy, the owner of the resthouse came across to them, thus saving her the need to answer.

'It's some time since you stayed a night, young Gavin,' he remarked. 'Would you mind if the wife and I joined you for dinner? We don't get much company and she's always telling me that we ought to retire and go and live in Colombo.' Gavin avoided Patsy's eyes as he answered.

'By all means come and eat with us. Let me introduce you to Miss Marley, who came back with me from England to look after Rory 's little girl. Patsy this is Mr Blake —'

'Just Tom, please,' the man said, holding out a brown hand. 'I heard about that, Gavin. A bad business. How is the little lass settling down out here?'

'Thanks to Miss Marley, very well.'

They were soon joined by Tom's wife, a grey-haired woman of about sixty, who looked as if she had been very pretty when she was younger, and a Singhalese servant brought in the excellent meal.

The evening passed quickly, and Patsy sat

mostly quiet as she listened to the conversation of the others. At about ten-thirty, Gavin asked for 'a last nightcap' and after Tom had brought it, Patsy and Gavin were left alone to drink it.

'It's been a lovely day,' Patsy said, 'and I don't know whether Tanya or I enjoyed it more.'

'I probably enjoyed it more than either of you,' he rejoined. 'You're a very good companion, Patsy.' They finished their drinks, and Patsy went off to bed, leaving him to say his last goodnights to his host.

'A very good companion,' she thought a little bitterly in the privacy of the room she was sharing with Tanya. 'I wish I could be more than that to you, my darling.' She lay for a while thinking about this day they had passed together, before sleep claimed her and she dreamt happily of similar happy days.

At breakfast Gavin said that they would go up once more to watch the elephants for a little while, and perhaps have another brief swim, and then they would eat the picnic lunch which Tom's wife was preparing for them, and head back to Colombo. This time they eagerly looked forward to what they knew they would see: the monkeys, the wonderful flowers and the huge butterflies, and of course the elephants. Too soon the morning was over, and they were saying goodbye to Sunderaja and getting into Gavin's car for the journey home. They were quiet on the way, each busy with thoughts of their own. When they reached the house Gavin carried in the cases and then said:

'I must go to the office. Elaine will want to tell me what, if anything, has been going on while we were away. I'll bring her back to dinner. Will you tell Mrs Jancsz?'

Patsy agreed with a slight sinking of her heart. She didn't want the other girl to intrude yet on the little shining bubble of intimacy that she had enjoyed with Gavin and Tanya. 'But I've had it,' she told herself, 'and now I expect life will get back to normal.'

Tanya had woken up a bit now that they were home, and she, too, obviously wanted to keep alive the memory of the past two days, for she urged Patsy to write at once in her diary about the monkeys and the elephants and all they had seen and done. 'I'll draw some pictures and we can stick them in,' she planned. The rest of the afternoon was spent in this way, and when Gavin came home again Tanya was, as usual, ready for bed and already feeling sleepy. He came alone and for a moment Patsy's heart lifted, until he said:

'Elaine is following. She had a few letters she wanted to type before she left.'

They went through the usual evening ritual of having a drink with the child and then Gavin went off to shower and change, and Patsy to read to Tanya and put her to bed.

Tanya only wanted to hear what Patsy had written about their trip, and then she settled down for the night. She was asleep almost before her head touched the pillow, and Patsy stood looking down at her for a few minutes before she ran a comb through her curls, put on fresh lipstick and went downstairs. It was already dusk but the lights had not yet been lit. As she approached the drawing-room which led to the verandah, she became aware of the silhouette of two people in the doorway, with their arms tightly wrapped around each other and their lips together. She stopped as if she had been hit, and unconsciously one hand went to her heart. Gavin and Elaine. The little cocoon of happiness in which she had been wrapped suddenly fell away. Gavin thought her a good companion, but now he was back with his love, and it was like a physical blow to see them together.

As she stood rooted to the spot she heard a slight sound behind her, and looking round she saw Gavin coming round the bend in the stairs. She just stared at him, unable to think of anything to say. He ran lightly down and joined her. 'Almost a dead heat,' he said cheerfully. Patsy said nothing, but turned again to look towards the silhouette in the doorway. The lights were on and there was no silhouette! Instead, Elaine stood by the bar and smiled towards them.

'I was just going to get myself a drink,

darling,' she said, 'but now that you're here you can do it for me.' She smiled briefly at Patsy but otherwise ignored her, and went on chatting to Gavin. Patsy sank into a chair and accepted her drink from him, glad to be silent and to try to cope with the chaos of her thoughts. It had not been Gavin! Who was it then? And where was he now? Before long her questions seemed answered, but the answer left her mind in even more of a turmoil.

'My car's broken down,' Elaine complained. 'Peter brought me over. Will you take me home later?'

Peter! It could only have been Elaine's brother with her in the doorway. Patsy tried to think what it could mean but Gavin was drawing her determinedly into the conversation and she had to force her mind to concentrate on what was being said. Gavin took the other girl home fairly early, and Patsy escaped to her bedroom before he returned. Her thoughts went round in a circle. Perhaps she had imagined it—some trick of the light had made her see what was not there? Again and again she relived those few moments when she had felt so sick at what she had thought was the sight of Gavin kissing Elaine, but she got no nearer to an explanation, and at last she went wearily to bed.

In the morning it all seemed like a bad dream, and she tried to forget it. This was made easier by Gavin's suggestion at breakfast.

'I'm going out to the nearest plantation today with Elaine, to check up on some export orders,' he said. 'Would you like to come with us? You've seen where a plantation is going to be, but you haven't yet seen one in production. You might find it interesting.'

'Will there be elephants?' Tanya wanted to know.

'No, but there will be people picking tea leaves, and you can see the big machines at work, and the packing-shed.' Tanya lost interest but Patsy, clinging to any possible time spent with Gavin, and interested in anything that interested him, said that she would like to go.

'We'll pick Elaine up on the way,' Gavin said, but the phone rang before the end of the meal and Gavin came back to report that Elaine was going to take Peter's car and drive out, and that he would collect hers from the garage during the morning. Patsy's heart lifted a little, and a little more when she realised at the end of the drive that Elaine would be working in the office and not coming with them on their tour.

It was a perfect day. The sky was like a blue ceiling with no cloud in sight, and the whole plantation stretched out before them like a brightly-coloured travel poster. To the left of the office where they parked, there were long low buildings, in which Gavin told them the tea was prepared and packed, and ahead and to the right stretched what looked like miles of green bushes shining in the sun, whilst brightly-clad figures moved methodically up and down the rows. Gavin led them to a small jeep which stood nearby.

'We're always changing cars,' Tanya commented.

Gavin ruffled her hair. 'It's too hot for you to walk as far as we're going,' he explained. 'I want to drive to where some of the women are at the edge of a row so that you can watch what they are doing.'

'Women?' Patsy asked.

'Yes. All the pickers are women; the men work in the factory part of the business.'

He stopped the jeep after a while and they sat and watched the women work.

'They look like a flock of exotic birds,' Patsy exclaimed. 'How beautiful saris are.'

'I'll buy you one,' Gavin said. 'You can wear it at home. It would suit your dark eyes.' Patsy was silent. 'Wear it at home.' How cosy and belonging that sounded. She wondered briefly if he had ever bought a sari for Elaine. 'But she probably wouldn't wear one,' she thought, 'and anyhow she hasn't got dark eyes.' Irrationally comforted by this thought, she smiled at Gavin but did not accept his offer.

'The baskets are tied on their heads!' Tanya noticed with surprise.

'The Singhalese always carry loads like that,' her uncle told her. 'It leaves their hands

112

free for other things.'

'What other things?' Tanya asked at once.

'Well, for picking the tea leaves, to put in the basket. Watch and see how quickly they do it.'

They watched in silence for a few minutes, and Patsy was impressed by the ease and speed at which the women picked.

'We pick only the top new little leaves,' Gavin told them, 'and the bushes are continually producing more.'

The baskets were fastened round the women's heads with what looked like bright scarves. The colours often clashed with those of their saris, but as with a bunch of flowers the colours didn't seem to matter, the whole effect was so pleasing.

'Could I take a photograph?' Patsy asked. 'Would they mind?'

'I'm sure they wouldn't, but it would be courteous to ask them,' he replied. 'Come, let's go and see.' He helped them out of the jeep, and with Tanya clinging to Patsy's hand they walked a little way down one of the rows to the nearest woman. He greeted her and spoke to her briefly in a language which Patsy did not understand. Tanya looked at him in wonder. The woman said something with a giggle and turned to call to some others nearby who came at once to join her. Gavin greeted them all and then arranged them in a small group in front of the bushes. Patsy took her photographs and

113

then said thank you, hoping that they would understand what she meant by her tone if nothing else. One of the women spoke shyly to Gavin and he answered her with a smile.

'Would the little one like to pick some tea?' he translated.

They both looked at the child, expecting her to be too shy, but Tanya held up her arms to Gavin and said, 'Yes, please.'

He picked her up and carried her to the nearest bush.

'Pick just the tiny little leaves at the very top,' he told her, 'and put them in the basket.' Patsy took another photograph as the leaves were duly picked, and then Tanya wriggled to be put down. Gavin thanked the women and they went back to the jeep.

'It doesn't look like tea,' Tanya observed. 'Tea is sort of brown colour.'

'Observant child!' He smiled at them both. 'That's right. Those green leaves get dried and ground. We'll go to the sheds now and you can see it being done.'

Patsy would have liked to stay longer and watch the process of tea-making, but Tanya soon lost interest, and the dust seemed to make her sneeze, so their tour was brief.

'Now we'll go to the office and have a cup of tea,' Gavin announced as they came out into the sunshine again. 'You mustn't expect a cup of coffee on a tea plantation.'

'You're back quickly.' Elaine greeted them

almost irritably, Patsy thought.

'Yes,' Gavin said briefly. 'How about some tea?'

Elaine called and another sari-clad figure came through from an adjoining room. 'Tea,' she said and the soft-footed woman went away to prepare it. 'We've got two parties today,' Elaine went on to say to Gavin.

'Good,' he smiled. 'It all helps, I suppose.' And turning to Patsy, he explained, 'This plantation has become something of a showplace, and we often have groups of tourists coming to look over it.' He pointed to one side of the room, to where lots of very miniature tea-chests were stacked.

'Visitors can buy these little souvenir boxes of tea straight from the plantation,' he said. 'We address them to wherever they're going and they're sent off with our regular export orders.'

'What a good idea.'

'Would you like to send some?' he asked as the woman returned with a tea-tray.

'Yes please,' Patsy replied, thinking of her colleague Sue, and of Jan and Peter whose house she had shared.

'Just give Elaine the addresses then, and she'll see to it.'

They drank their tea and then Gavin, glancing at his watch, said that he'd better take them back to Colombo. Tanya was tugging at his sleeve, and he bent to hear her low voice.

'Uncle Gavin, may I have one of the pretty little boxes?'

'Of course,' he said at once, reaching across to take a small tea-chest from Elaine's desk. 'A memento of your visit.' He gave her the box, and got up from his chair.

'That's not a very nice one,' Elaine said, also getting to her feet. 'Here, Tanya, this one is better.'

The child clutched the box which Gavin had given her more firmly.

'I like this one,' she said stubbornly. Patsy sighed. 'Even when Elaine makes some effort, Tanya won't meet her halfway,' she thought. 'How will those two ever get on together?'

'OK. You keep that one then,' Gavin said cheerfully. 'Come on, let's go.'

He left them at the house with a wave and they sat on the verandah and talked about the morning.

'Will you write about it?' Tanya wanted to know.

'If you like, and you must soon learn to write so that you can write about things as well.'

'All right,' Tanya agreed doubtfully, 'but now I'd like to put some decorate on my box.'

'You want to decorate your tea-chest? Well that's a good idea,' Patsy agreed. 'Use your felt-tip pens. They'll show up better.'

CHAPTER TEN

With a protruding tongue and fierce concentration Tanya set about making patterns in bright colours on the sides of the little box. Lunch was ready when she had finished three sides, but she left it quite happily and agreed with Patsy that she could finish it after her afternoon rest. Patsy went up with her and after writing about the events of the morning, she too dozed a little in the heat of the afternoon. The sound of a car on the gravel below her window awoke her, and at first she took no notice, thinking that perhaps it was a delivery of some kind. She lay for a while, half awake and half asleep, and then realising that she hadn't heard the car leave, she got up to peep out of the window. Perhaps Gavin had come back early. To her disappointment she saw that Elaine's car stood there. What could she be here for? Patsy lingered for a little while, not wanting to go down, but then thinking that perhaps Gavin had asked her to come for some reason, she washed her face, combed her hair and put on fresh lipstick before she went to see. Elaine was sitting on the settee, and to Patsy she seemed to be a bit breathless.

'Are you all right?' she asked involuntarily.

Elaine nodded and smiled. 'I just felt a bit

giddy,' she admitted. 'I think I've been rushing about too much. I came for some papers that Gavin left in his study.'

Patsy nodded. 'You'd better get them,' she said. 'I won't know which they are. But can I get you a drink or something?'

Elaine shook her head. 'I'm in rather a hurry.' She got up hastily and left the room. Patsy turned to tidy away the little tea-chest and all the felt-tip pens which Tanya had left on the settee, and suddenly she sat perfectly still. The tea-chest which lay there now was not the one that Tanya had brought home! The scrawls and patterns looked the same, but Patsy, who had been urged to admire them in detail, knew that they were slightly different. She remembered in a flash how Elaine had not wanted the child to bring that particular box. 'She must have come here to change them! But why?' She glanced at Elaine's very large handbag which lay beside her on the settee. On impulse, after a hasty glance towards the door, she unzipped the bag. There inside was the original tea-chest! With hardly a thought, Patsy quickly exchanged the two boxes and had just pulled the zip when Elaine hurried in.

'I forgot my bag!' she exclaimed. With a fast-beating heart, but outwardly calm, Patsy replied as lightly as she could:

'Well, it's safe enough here.'

'I—I want a phone number from it,' Elaine said hastily, and taking the bag she went again from the room. Patsy waited in an agony of apprehension. After a very few minutes she heard the slight ring as the telephone was put down and then Elaine swept through the room again.

'Well, I'll get back,' she said, and Patsy bade her goodbye. She sat like a statue until the last sounds of Elaine's car had died away, and then with slightly trembling hands she took the little chest and went up to her room. This chest looked exactly like all the others; what was there that made Elaine go to such lengths to get it back? She had been lucky to find the drawing-room empty and the box lying there. She had probably hoped just to be able to take it when she had a chance. It must have been a blow to see that the box had been scribbled on, but the pens were there, and she was able to duplicate the other box she had obviously brought with her. Only she had not quite duplicated it; very nearly, but not quite. Patsy looked at the original box she now held in her shaking hands. In all ways it was the same as all the other boxes; there must be something inside it. She peeped in on Tanya, who was still sound asleep, and then with her nail-file she prised off the lid of the box. It was not easy, and she cut her finger on the fancy tin-work which bound the top and bottom of it, but at last the top was off and she looked eagerly at the contents.

Tea! That was what was in it. Tea—just as it

should have been. Patsy felt a great sense of anticlimax. 'But Elaine wouldn't have wanted it back if it only contained tea,' she thought, and picking up a magazine from her bedside table she spread it across her knees and slowly poured the tea-leaves from the chest. In the next second she gave a great gasp. Among the grey of the contents she suddenly saw gleaming green. Her hands shook a little more as she picked them out. 'Emeralds!' she whispered. And as she collected them together, the full realisation of what this must mean flooded over her. All those little chests were destined to be sent abroad. They would go with all the rest of the tea and no-one would ever know that the jewels lay hidden there. Elaine must be engaged in smuggling jewels out of the country! Elaine and Peter. Quickly her mind made the connection. Peter dealt with precious stones. He was in an ideal position to receive stolen or doubtfully acquired jewels, and Elaine was in an ideal position to get them out of the country. After a stunned moment or two she tried to decide what to do. She must tell Gavin at once, she thought. Halfway down the stairs she changed her mind. If she phoned Gavin, perhaps Elaine would answer the phone. It would be better to wait until he came home. She looked at her watch. What a long time it seemed to wait. Should she go to the police? Better not, she thought. It would take ages to explain it all,

120

and perhaps there would be some language difficulty. Gavin would be able to deal with it all, but how on earth was she going to fill in the time until he came home, and what if Elaine came with him as she so often did. She would somehow have to occupy Tanya, she realised; the child would want to continue with her decoration and could not be allowed to see the opened box. On impulse she took out her diary and wrote a hasty account of all that had happened. 'My mind feels like a whirlpool at the moment,' she thought. 'At least I'll get things down as they happened.' Tanya slept on, and Patsy went downstairs with the box and its precious contents in her hands to put it in Gavin's desk.

She got just as far as the hallway before she was confronted by Peter and Elaine who came hurriedly in through the open doorway. They looked at the box in her hands.

'You've opened it,' Peter stated rather than asked, and turning to Elaine he said angrily, 'Why did you have to phone to say you'd changed them? That must have given her time to change them over again.'

His face was white with anger. Elaine was cooler.

'I thought you'd be anxious to know,' she said. 'But that's not important now. What are we going to do?'

'We need time.' Peter grabbed Patsy's arm and half dragged her to Gavin's study, where

121

he pushed both women inside and stood with his back to the door. 'She mustn't be able to tell.'

'Peter!' For once Elaine seemed to lose her calm manner.

'Oh don't be stupid,' he said impatiently. 'I won't do her any harm. We're in enough trouble as it is if we don't get away. She's just got to be put away somewhere long enough for us to get out.' He turned to Patsy.

'You'll come with us,' he said flatly.

Patsy's voice trembled. 'I won't,' she said.

'Oh yes you will. Your housekeeper is no doubt having her afternoon sleep, the servants are off-duty until this evening, and we are both stronger than you are. Come without a fuss and you won't get hurt. We'll just stow you away somewhere where you won't be found for a couple of days.'

'If you don't come willingly we'll take the kid as well,' Elaine put in, and looking from one to the other Patsy knew that they were in deadly earnest. Peter thought for a minute, then with a half chuckle he said.

'Sit down there and write a note to Gavin and tell him that you've gone away with me,' he commanded. 'He surprised me kissing you the other night. He'll believe it for long enough for us to leave Sri Lanka.' He pushed her towards the desk and Patsy thought desperately of what she might be able to put in the note to give Gavin some inkling that all was not well. As if he read her thoughts Peter said roughly, 'Don't try to be clever, just write, "Dear Gavin, I've gone away with Peter. Please don't try to make me come back." And sign your name.' Feeling completely helpless, Patsy did as he commanded. There was nothing else that she could do. It was true that the servants were always free from lunch time until teatime, and true too that Mrs Jancsz would probably be deeply asleep, and even if she were not they would hustle her into the car and away before she could cry for help or explain what was happening.

'Put it in an envelope and write his name on it, and we'll leave it on the desk.' Patsy obeyed. Although she was afraid, she felt more worried about Tanya than she did about herself. What would the child do when she woke up and could not, as usual, see Patsy waiting for her? The note finished and propped up against his typewriter where Gavin would surely see it, Peter again grabbed Patsy roughly by the arm.

'Now no fuss,' he warned her. 'Neither you nor the kid nor anyone else will come to any harm if you just do as you're told.'

They went through the door and turned to leave the house, but they were stopped by a small complaining voice.

'Patsy. You weren't there when I woke up.'

Halfway down the stairs Tanya stood looking down at them. All three froze for a second, and then Elaine muttered:

'We'll have to take her.'

'No!' Patsy found her voice, and turning towards the still sleepy child, she said in a voice as cool as she could make it:

'I'm sorry I wasn't there, darling, and I'm afraid I have to go out now with Peter.'

'Can I come?' Tanya descended another two steps.

'No,' Patsy said hastily. 'You can't come this time. Go to the kitchen and wait for Mrs Jancsz and tell her I said you were to stay with her until Uncle Gavin comes home.'

'Clothes!' Elaine said suddenly, and Peter nodded his head.

'Get them,' he said tersely, 'but hurry.' Elaine nodded and ran up the shallow stairs. Peter turned again to Patsy. 'Will that kid do as she's told?' he demanded roughly.

'Yes of course.' Patsy tried to keep her voice calm. 'Tanya, in a minute go to the kitchen and wait for Mrs Jancsz. She won't be long. She might already be there. Tell her and tell Uncle Gavin that I've gone with Peter. Uncle Gavin will put you to bed and he'll read you a story like I do. Ask him to read to you about the elephants. Now off you go, there's a good girl.'

To her relief the child did not object any more but went slowly off towards the kitchen. As soon as her back was turned Peter hustled Patsy out to the waiting car, and pushed her into the back seat. He stood tapping his foot impatiently until Elaine appeared, carrying

124

one of Patsy's suitcases.

'I didn't stop for everything,' she said, 'but it'll look perfectly normal to have taken just what I have taken.' She thrust Patsy's handbag into the back of the car.

'Where's your passport?' Peter demanded.

'It's in Gavin's desk.'

'Get it,' he snapped, and again Elaine went off at a run. Patsy sat very straight in the back seat, determined not to let them see that she was frightened. She tried not to imagine Gavin's home-coming. What would he think? What would he do?

'Where are you taking me?' she asked, as at last the car moved down the drive with Elaine on the back seat beside her.

'Shut up!' Peter told her angrily, and there was silence as he threaded his way through the Colombo traffic. Elaine kept looking behind her as if she thought they might be followed, and Patsy guessed that she was badly shaken by all that had happened.

'You won't get away with it!' she said, thinking that if she could add to Elaine's concern they might get careless and perhaps somehow she could get away.

'I said shut up!' Peter repeated, and drove a little faster.

'Be careful,' Elaine warned. 'We don't want an accident.'

'You be quiet too. It's all your fault that this happened at all.'

Elaine noticed a small look of triumph on Patsy's face, and said in a milder tone:

'Well it has happened, and we've just got to cope with it. Where are we going now?'

'Home,' he told her curtly. 'I'll stay in the car with our guest, and you go in and pack for us. Bring passports and any money that is there.'

Elaine seemed to take a long time to do his bidding, and sitting beside Patsy in the back seat with his hand grasping her arm, Peter evidently spent it in planning, for when she came out with two suitcases he said:

'I've had a better idea. Put those cases in the back of my car, and you stay here. Drive over to Gavin's place so that you arrive just after he does, and you can be surprised and shocked with him. It'll be much more authentic like that. I'll come back here and do any last-minute things, and you can leave Gavin pretty soon and join me here. Luckily we've got plenty of cash. We'll go to the airport and take any plane that's going. We can make further plans later.' Elaine stood beside the car and looked at him.

'How do I know I can trust you, Peter?' she said slowly with narrowed eyes. 'You've been getting restless for a long time. How do I know you won't just go off and leave me here?'

He leaned out from the back seat to look at her.

'Darling, we've seen too much together for me to leave you,' he said. 'Surely you know I wouldn't leave you? But if you like you can take both passports with you as insurance.'

'I think I'll do that,' Elaine replied. 'I don't much like the idea of going back to see Gavin, though I do see the sense in it, but I will take both passports just in case anything goes wrong and you panic.'

'When have you ever known me to panic?' he countered angrily. 'Put the bags in the back and let me get off.'

'Where are you taking her?'

'To Ranji's place,' Peter told her tersely as he forced Patsy out of the back seat and into the front one. 'He's involved in all this, even though only in a small way. He'll agree to keep her.'

As the cases were put into the back, Patsy looked desperately around for someone to whom she could shout for help, but there was no-one about, and even if there had been she knew that Peter would have driven away before she could make anyone believe that she was in real trouble.

'Don't get any clever ideas about trying to jump out,' Peter warned her as he started the car again. 'I'll be driving fast and you'd only get hurt; I should just drive away and leave you and it would take Gavin just as long to find you in a hospital.'

Patsy made no reply. Her fear was giving way to frustration that she knew their plans but was quite helpless to do anything about it.

CHAPTER ELEVEN

They drove for a long time and the beautiful houses with their green lawns and neat drives gave way to bad roads and neglected looking shacks. Patsy felt utterly helpless and her fear returned.

'You won't get away, you know,' she said, trying to hang on to her dwindling courage so that at least Peter wouldn't see how frightened she really was.

'We'll be out of the country and far away before anyone knows what it's all about,' he replied with a malicious smile. 'Think yourself lucky that I'm only putting you in storage for a while. We had a sweet thing going, and you've spoilt it for us.'

'You said you were getting restless. Elaine was careless, perhaps you would soon have got careless too,' Patsy said bravely, hoping to goad him into further revelations, but Peter didn't answer. At last they stopped before a house that looked better kept than the others and he drew the car to a skidding halt. He held his hand on the horn and a man dressed in a sarong and a white shirt came out with a puzzled look on his face.

'We've been discovered,' Peter told him curtly. 'You'll be all right if you carry on as usual and keep your head, but we've got to leave in a hurry.'

'But what? Why?—' The man looked bewildered and frightened at the same time.

'There's no time for explanations. She—' Peter jerked his head towards Pasty, 'has found out too much, and she's got to be kept out of the way in order to give us time to get away.'

'But what do you mean, how can—'

'Oh, don't be stupid, man!' Peter interrupted furiously. 'I told you. She's found out about us, but nobody else knows, and if she's held here for a time we can get off the island.'

'But what about me?'

'There's no need for you to be implicated at all. Your best bet would be to keep right on as you are, nobody's going to suspect you; but if you want to leave you'd better go far and fast. What I'm saying is that she's got to be out of circulation for some time to give us time. Until about this time tomorrow.'

'You want me to keep her here?'

Peter clenched his fists. 'Heaven preserve me from idiots! Yes! She can be shut in here somewhere and you can let her out at this time tomorrow. If you want to leave now I'm sure you can pay someone to keep his mouth shut and to come and let her out.' He leapt out of the car and crossed to the passenger side. 'Out,' he commanded briefly, holding open the door. Patsy got out.

The other man was clasping and unclasping

his hands. 'But it is so sudden,' he wailed. 'Arrangements have to be made.'

'That's your affair. As I told you, you can go or ride it out. You'll be OK. We're the ones at risk. Now come on; which room here can we lock her in?'

The dark-skinned man pulled himself together with a visible effort.

'There is a store-room,' he said. 'It has a lock, but no window. I—'

'All the better,' Peter interrupted maliciously. 'She won't hurt in there for twenty-four hours. It'll be uncomfortable, but I'm certainly not interested in her comfort.' Briefly Patsy thought of trying to run, but she guessed that it would be useless. Both men could certainly run faster that she could, and in this district she guessed that whatever went on people would not interfere, and no-one would help her. Peter propelled her up the two rickety steps to the small verandah and into the tiny house.

'In here.' The other man slipped ahead of them and opened a door. Patsy caught a glimpse of sacks of what she supposed were rice. As the man had said, there was no window, and as far as she could see nothing else except the sacks. For a moment panic gripped her and she tried to wrench free from Peter's restraining hand. He tightened it cruelly and pushed her violently into the little room. The door slammed behind her and she heard their receding voices. The little room was not as dark as she had expected it to be. The door did not fit well, and dusty sunlight showed round its edges. She realised that the daylight would soon be gone and then it would be dark indeed. Her spirit quailed at the thought of being shut up there for twenty-four hours, and as she heard Peter's car drive away she succumbed to panic and beat loudly on the door with her fists.

'Let me out,' she shouted. 'I will pay you if you will let me out and I will forget that I ever saw you.' There was no answer, though she could hear sounds of movement beyond the door. For a time she kept up her banging and shouting, but it soon became obvious that it was useless. Summoning all her resolves of will-power, she told herself that there was no way of escape and that she must endure this incarceration as best she could.

In the little light that came through the badly fitting door she looked around her. She was in just a bare wooden room, with, as the man had said, no window. Light came through a few cracks between the wooden boards, but she soon saw that she would have no hope of loosening any of them. There were four sacks and two small boxes which she guessed from the smell contained dried fish. With a sigh and a drooping of her shoulders she realised that there was nothing she could do but wait. She sat on one of the sacks and tried to relax. She could just see the hands of her watch and knew that it would be at least another hour until Gavin reached home. She wondered about Tanya. Poor baby! She had looked so lost and alone as they had left. What would Mrs Jancsz think at the child's explanation that she had left with Peter? And what would Gavin think when he found her note?

What could she have done to have avoided being in this situation? Peter and Elaine were too strong for her, and besides they had threatened to take Tanya as well. Her thoughts wandered over Gavin and the child and the time she had spent here in Sri Lanka with them. The little girl had blossomed into a carefree child, and Gavin treated her as if he had always been used to having a small child in the house. For a while her thoughts just roamed aimlessly, and then as the tiny room grew dimmer she looked once more at her watch. She had been there only an hour, and soon it would be dark and she would not even be able to see what time it was. Once more she tried banging on the door and shouting, but there was no response at all, and when she stopped and listened she heard no sound at all and she guessed that she was entirely alone. For a panicky moment she wondered about rats, but there was no sound at all and she hoped and prayed that she would hear no evidence of them.

She thought of stories she had read of

prisoners-of-war put into solitary confinement, and how they had passed the time and kept their sanity. 'I'm not in nearly such an awful situation as they were,' she told herself. 'I've just got to occupy my thoughts for some hours. Perhaps I'll even sleep.' But she didn't sleep and the hours seemed to creep by with agonising slowness. She tried to guess at the time but felt terrible frustration at the thought that it was most probably not nearly as late as she thought it was. She felt very hot and thirsty, and tried to keep her mind off long cool drinks. At last she thought only of Gavin. She remembered him as she had first seen him, crouching beside Tanya and trying to interest the child in what was in the toy-shop window. She thought of the first dinner they had had together, and how he had told her about himself. She relived the two days they had spent together with Tanya in England before they had flown to Sri Lanka, and she went over everything that she could remember of her time here in his house. 'I think I fell in love with him during those first few days,' she told herself, 'and since I've been here with him it's just been growing and growing.' She wondered how all this would affect him. What would he feel when he learned about the real Elaine? Did he love her very much? She imagined Elaine going to the house just after Gavin got home, to be, as Peter had said, 'shocked and surprised with him'. However well she played that part, and Patsy imagined that she could do it very well, there would still be no future for Gavin with Elaine. Again she wondered what time it was, and then angry with herself for such futile wondering, she determined that she wouldn't think about the time any more, and she went back to thoughts of Gavin, until she felt that she had relived every moment since she had first met him. Sitting on a sack of rice, she leaned back against the hard wooden wall and tried to doze. 'If I could sleep a little it would help to pass the time,' she thought, but she remained maddeningly wide awake.

Suddenly she was pulled back to the present with a jerk. A car came to a screeching halt outside. She sat up straight, her heart suddenly beating faster. She heard hurried footsteps on the wooden floor outside and she was instantly on her feet, her hands clasped tightly by her side.

'Patsy! Where are you, Patsy?' It was Gavin's voice and her heart gave a great leap of joy.

'Here!' she called, banging again on the door. 'I'm in here.'

Again came his voice. 'OK. Stand well away from the door.' Patsy retreated to the far side of the little room and in the next minute the lock gave way under Gavin's kicks and he hurtled into the room. It was quite dark, but she felt his hands reaching for her, and heard his anxious voice. 'Are you all right, Patsy? They didn't hurt you, did they?'

'I'm all right,' she told him with a shaky attempt at a laugh. 'Just tired of being in this room. What time is it?'

'I'm not sure. About ten o'clock I think.'

'I've only been here a few hours,' Patsy marvelled. 'It feels like days.'

'Let's get home,' Gavin urged, leading her carefully out, down the rickety steps and into the dark road. 'What you need is a good strong drink, and we can do all our talking later.' Although the night was warm Patsy shivered a little as they went. He put out a hand and briefly touched her knee.

'You've had a shock,' he said, 'but you'll be all right when we get home.'

No more was said and the big car rushed smoothly through the dark streets. Red was waiting for them on the verandah and he ran down the few steps and enfolded Patsy in a bear-hug as soon as she stepped from the car. His voice was not quite steady as he held her away from him and demanded, 'Are you all right? They didn't hurt you, did they? Oh, Patsy, I've been out of my mind with worry.' Gavin came quietly round the front of the car.

'Let's go inside. Patsy could do with a strong drink, and I daresay both of us could use one as well.' Patsy began to shake even more as she realised that her ordeal was truly over and that she was safely back at home. With his arm still around her shoulders, Red led her inside and she sank gratefully on to the settee.

'Where did you find her?' Red asked.

'In the house in the old quarter where Ranji lives. I don't suppose you know him; he was employed at the plantation and was evidently to some extent in on this whole business,' Gavin answered, busy at the bar.

'Here you are,' he went on, crossing to Patsy with a glass in his hand. 'It's not what you usually have, but I think that right now a brandy is what you need.' Patsy gasped as the strong liquid hit her throat and Gavin mixed drinks for himself and Red, but soon her shivering stopped, and she looked from one to the other of the men with a shaky smile.

'What happened?' Red demanded then. 'You gave me the barest details on the phone, and then told me to alert the police and go to Peter's house, and if he was there to get out of him where he had taken Patsy. I did that but before I could get anything out of him Elaine arrived in near hysterics. She said that you had made her tell where Patsy was, and that you were on your way to get her; so I came back here. When I left they were hurling accusations at each other. I don't think they even saw me go.'

Gavin sipped his drink and told Red all that had led up to the events of the evening.

'I got home,' he said, 'to find Tanya in tears and Mrs Jancsz thoroughly puzzled. She said that she had found Tanya in the kitchen, crying, with a story of Patsy having told her that she was going with Peter. Then I found this note on my desk.' He fumbled in his pocket for the crumpled letter, and passed it to Red.

'They made you write it,' he assumed, as he read the few sentences. Patsy nodded.

'They said if I didn't come willingly they would take Tanya as well.'

'Then what happened?' Red turned again to Gavin.

'Mrs Jancsz had got Tanya ready for bed, so I tried to comfort her a little and then took her upstairs. Elaine arrived just then, and I told her I'd be down in a very little while. When we got upstairs Tanya said that you had told her to ask me to read to her about the elephants. I was longing to get downstairs and find out what Elaine knew, but I thought I'd better just read a little bit, so I asked her to get me whichever book that particular story was in. To my surprise she got a plain exercise book from under Patsy's pillow. "Patsy wrote about them and about the monkeys," she told me, and I realised that it must be some kind of a diary of events. As she gave it to me it fell open at the last entry and the first thing I saw was, "Elaine and Peter have been smuggling jewels out of the country in little tea-chests." Poor Tanya waited in vain for her story as I quickly read the rest. Then I phoned you, Red, from the bedroom, got Mrs Jancsz to come and sit with Tanya who was crying again, and went down stairs to Elaine. She acted very well, I must say. She came towards me with a worried look on her face saying, "Oh Gavin, is it true?" She had a bad shock when I grabbed her arm and said, "You're going to tell me what's true." And I forced her down on to the settee. She tried to bluff at first, but she soon realised that I already knew too much, and then she tried to leave. I hung on to her and for some reason I took her handbag, perhaps I thought there might be some clue as to where Patsy was. I wasn't thinking too clearly. I was too worried and too angry. However, I saw the two passports in her bag and took them.'

'Poor Elaine!' Patsy giggled weakly. 'That's the second time today that she had something taken from her handbag.'

'Elaine was still trying to get away and I told her that I would let her leave, but that a charge of kidnapping on top of everything else would only make matters worse and she suddenly collapsed and told me where Patsy was.'

They looked round at each other in satisfaction, and suddenly Patsy gave a huge yawn. Red jumped to his feet.

'I'm going,' he said. 'I guess you need a hot bath, something to eat, and then a nice long sleep. I'll see you tomorrow. Goodnight, both.' He bent and kissed the top of Patsy's head and then was gone.

'I think I've just lived through the worst hours of my life,' Gavin said, and there was a little silence. Patsy picked up her diary which was lying on the settee where Gavin had left it. At last he said slowly:

'Are you in love with Red, Patsy? It's very obvious that he's in love with you.'

Patsy shook her head.

'I like him a lot, but I'm not in love with him. He asked me to marry him.'

These was another small pause before she asked:

'You didn't really believe that I could have run off with Peter, did you?'

'With the evidence of your note I thought it was just possible. I did come home unexpectedly early to find you kissing him, but if you want him I couldn't see why you had to leave in such a way.'

'He was kissing me,' Patsy corrected. 'I was struggling to get away from him. I thought I quite liked him before that.' She in her turn asked a question:

'Are you very upset about Elaine? I mean I know you're in love with her and this must have—'

'I am not in love with Elaine,' he interrupted, 'so finding out what she's been up to, and also from the passports that she is Peter's wife, not his sister, did nothing at all to my feelings. I used to like her a lot. She was good company, and very decorative, and I

139

thought that one day I might ask her to marry me, but that was before you came into my life.'

Patsy looked at him, her heart beating fast.

'I think I must have loved you right from those first few days in England,' he said, crossing swiftly to sit by her side. 'I wanted to tell you long before this but I was afraid I would be taking an unfair advantage of you. You were here, away from all possible boyfriends that you might have had in England, and I—'

'Is that why you insisted that I should have more free time to go out with Red or Peter or anyone else?'

'Yes. I hated doing it, and I grabbed the chance to have you all to myself when they started clearing the ground for a new plantation. Oh Patsy, I love you so much. Will you marry me? Darling, please say you will.'

For answer she turned towards him and put her arms round his neck and her lips to his. For a while they both forgot everything but the importance of the moment. At last Patsy stirred and leaned back with her head against his shoulder. He kissed her hair.

'Thank God you were clever enough to give me a message through your diary.' His arms tightened round her. 'I hate to think of how long you might have been there otherwise.'

Patsy struggled to sit up. She picked up her diary and turned to him with a tremulous smile.

'There's another message for you in my diary,' she told him, and riffling through its pages she found and showed him where, so long ago it seemed, she had written, 'I love Gavin O'Rourke'.

We hope you have enjoyed this Large Print book. Other Chivers Press or G.K. Hall & Co. Large Print books are available at your library or directly from the publishers.

For more information about current and forthcoming titles, please call or write, without obligation, to:

Chivers Press Limited
Windsor Bridge Road
Bath BA2 3AX
England
Tel. (01225) 335336

OR

G.K. Hall & Co.
P.O. Box 159
Thorndike, Maine 04986
USA
Tel. (800) 223-2336

All our Large Print titles are designed for easy reading, and all our books are made to last.